The Sea View Cottage Conspiracy

*

The Lady Jane & Mrs Forbes Mysteries

Book Two

B. D. CHURSTON

ISBN: 9798851622120

One

June 1928

On a stormy Tuesday morning in Sandham-on-Sea, Kate Forbes and Lady Jane Scott hurried into the sparsely populated Promenade Tea Rooms.

"Phew!" gasped Kate. "One more gust and we'd have been blown to France."

"Lady Jane!" exclaimed Winnie Harris, the owner, from behind the counter. "How are you? It's been ages!"

Ages? Kate put her handbag down to shake off her umbrella. It had only been four months since Jane's last visit. Then again, news from afar was oxygen to the locals.

"I'm fine, thanks, Mrs Harris," said Jane as she tucked a wayward strand of auburn hair behind her ears. "I trust you're well?"

"Yes, very well, thank you."

"I love the new décor." Jane was indicating the fresh sunrise yellow walls and the giant potted aspidistra now filling a previously barren corner of the spacious seafront premises.

With warm brown eyes and a kindly face, this intelligent twenty-six-year-old was happy to chat about almost anything. Indeed, she looked set to say more, but Winnie's sister, Enid Turpin came bustling in from the gale with a flushed face and an inside-out umbrella.

"Oh, what a to-do!"

"Yes, shocking weather," said Kate.

"Yes, but the to-do isn't the weather. My neighbour's gone missing."

"Missing? Are you sure?"

"Of course I'm sure." Enid wedged the useless brolly under her arm and removed her hat. "It's Norman West. He wasn't at home last night. I've asked the other neighbours, but no one's seen or heard anything."

"Have you tried the police?" asked Jane.

"Yes – old grumpy says he's not interested."

"Oh… right."

While Jane smiled sympathetically, Kate felt it was disrespectful to refer to Sergeant Jones in this way, even if it was often justified.

But Enid wasn't finished.

"He says it's a free country and people are at liberty to go off as they please."

"You mean he can't be bothered," said Winnie.

Kate knew Norman West quite well. For one thing, they were Friday afternoon library regulars. Indeed, last Friday they chatted about knee pain while he changed a Wilkie Collins and a Conan Doyle for a couple of Dorothy L. Sayers.

"I'm sure he'll turn up," she said, although Enid had already disappeared into the small staff room behind the counter where she would swap her drenched coat for an apron.

"Did you drive all the way from London?" Winnie asked Jane.

"No, I came down by train. I'm staying till Saturday."

"You poor girl. You're either up to your eyeballs in dusty old parchments or knee deep in a muddy hole. There's more to life, you know. You must tell us all your plans."

"Let's have our coffee first," said Kate, bringing Winnie's fishing expedition to a halt.

She winked at her niece. No doubt Winnie would have quickly shunted them away from Jane's historical and archaeological pursuits onto her cancelled engagement to a viscount. The resulting absence of a glorious summer wedding hadn't been forgotten, while there would be much pondering over the true ideal match for the daughter of the Earl of Oxley.

Removing their raincoats, Kate and Jane took a table by the window. Here, Kate wiggled her arms, pleased to be down to just a cream day dress and light green cardigan.

Jane also looked relieved to be down to a sleeveless, pale blue, daisy-patterned summer dress.

Kate peered out into the gloom.

"It won't last," said Jane, pulling a tissue from her shoulder bag to mop her brow.

Kate smiled. "I was thinking of the holidaymakers. Poor things."

"They should go to Brighton," said staunch curmudgeon Ernie Melton, an elderly gentleman in an ancient suit. He was sitting alone in the corner by the aspidistra with a cup of tea and a sticky bun. "Lots more to do there."

"Thank you, Mr Melton," said Kate, "but we have plenty on offer here."

"I say it as I see it," he said before taking a slurp of tea. "When my Ethel was alive, she respected my opinion. Nobody else does."

Kate supposed The Regal, Sandham's only picture house, would be busy. Then there was the Alhambra Theatre, although that was becoming less popular thanks to the ever-growing demand for moving pictures. But Ernie Melton had a point. There wasn't nearly enough going on in Sandham for visitors.

"They've got two piers at Brighton," he mused.

"I know," said Kate.

"Lots of hotels."

"Yes..."

"Plenty of picture houses."

"Indeed…"

"And more tea rooms than you can shake a stick at. Everything's better in Brighton."

"I once went to Bognor," said Winnie for no apparent reason.

"Bognor?" questioned Ernie. "I took my Ethel there once. Seven days and nights. She ended up utterly miserable. Bognor can do that."

Kate smiled as best she could.

"Are you going along to Wilson's, Mrs Forbes?" asked Winnie.

"A little later, yes."

Wilson's Auction Rooms was due to hold a sale of items from a country house on Friday, but pre-auction viewing had already begun.

"I was thinking of getting something for my parlour," said Winnie. "It could do with a touch of class."

"I'm thinking along the same lines," said Kate.

"As am I," said Ernie.

Enid Turpin arrived at their table with two coffees on a tray.

"Ah, lovely," said Jane.

"He's a nice old chap," said Enid.

Kate glanced from the tray to Ernie Melton and back to Enid.

"Who is?"

"Norman West."

"Oh… yes, absolutely."

"Always telling you where he's been and where he's going next."

"Yes, very much so," said Kate. "A friendly presence in Sandham since his arrival."

"Should we be worried?" Jane asked.

"Well, it's true he's not the outdoors type."

"He's retired," said Enid. "Worked in the gentlemen's outfitters at a department store in London. Very good with people. Kind, well mannered, always interested in others. The kind of chap you like to help in return."

"True," said Kate, recalling the time she made him a winter stew when he was struggling with a heavy cold. On arrival, she found that six other ladies had come up with the same idea.

"He could be in trouble," said Enid. "I mean, here's us inside, warm and safe, enjoying hot coffee… and somewhere outside, lost and alone, there's poor Mr West battling the elements."

"We don't know that for certain," said Kate.

"He's probably had an accident," said Ernie Melton. "Most likely fallen down, prone, in anguish, broken limbs, sort of thing."

"We don't know that either," said Kate.

"Perhaps you could pop round to his house," said Enid. "I have a spare key, but I don't like to pry."

"I'm sure I don't like to pry either," said Kate.

Enid smiled hopefully. "Perhaps we could pry together?"

Kate sighed. "Sergeant Jones is most probably right. Norman will no doubt turn up soon enough. Besides, Jane is with me for a well-earned rest, not to catch her death in the damp."

"Oh, but you solved that business at Linton Hall," said Enid.

"It's hardly the same thing," said Kate.

"Exactly!" said Ernie. "Finding Norman should be a lot easier."

Kate thought of throwing Ernie Melton into the street with a message to go and look himself, but that attractive vision fell away to be replaced by Enid's troubled visage.

"It might be serious, Mrs Forbes. And he's such a lovely chap. It's not like we'd be poking our noses in where they're not wanted."

Kate peered once more through the window to the blustery street. Being by the seaside was beneficial for one's health and having a tan was no longer associated with manual labour. But not today. She'd either catch pneumonia or go rusty.

"How about we think before we leap?" she suggested. "What do we know for certain? For my part, I saw him at the library on Friday afternoon."

"I saw him on Saturday morning," said Enid. "He was coming back from the baker's with a small loaf."

"He wasn't in church on Sunday," said Winnie Harris from the counter. "I'd have noticed him otherwise."

"Me too," said Kate.

"Are we saying he disappeared on Sunday morning then?" asked Winnie.

"No, we're saying he was last seen on Saturday," said Jane.

"You're forgetting Sunday afternoon," said Ernie Melton.

"In what way?" said Kate.

"He went for a walk. Came right by my window."

"Any idea where he was going?"

"No, I never poke my nose into other people's business."

"I do hope nothing peculiar's happened," said Enid.

"I'm sure it's nothing," said Kate. "Although I don't suppose it would hurt for someone to take a look."

Ernie sniffed. "What rotten weather for you to contend with."

"Don't worry about us," said Kate. "It's the sailors at sea we should pray for."

"Most apt," said Ernie. "I'm having cod and chips for lunch."

Kate found his attempt at humour quite unnecessary. That said, cod and chips for lunch sounded spot on.

"Should I get my coat?" Enid wondered.

Kate looked forlornly at her coffee and then apologetically at her niece.

"Jane? Would you mind if we popped round to Norman's? It's only a fifteen-minute walk."

"Not at all, Aunt. As you say, it's probably nothing."

Two

Sandham-on-Sea began life as a 10th century Saxon settlement. With easy access to the sea and a natural harbour, fishing as much as agriculture dominated its history. The current town, however, dated mainly from the Georgian and Victorian periods where a wider array of commercial interests had slowly brought about the decline of the fishing fleet. For Kate, the town's next step was clear – attract more visitors and all would benefit.

"Poor Mr West," said Enid as they headed up a largely empty Royal Avenue, home to many small hotels and lodging houses. "It's such a worry."

"At least the rain's stopped," said Kate. "I'm sure, once the weather settles, we'll be inundated with visitors. What do you think, Enid?"

"He's never gone missing before."

"No, indeed…"

"Does he ever take trips away from home?" Jane asked.

Enid shook her head. "Not without letting his cleaner or me know. It's most unusual."

"I'm sure we'll learn something at his house," said Kate.

"A note or something," said Jane. "It's possible it was a last-minute thing."

"I doubt it," said Enid as they turned right onto the High Street, which was a little busier than Royal Avenue. "He's not a last-minute kind of man. Very meticulous, he is."

It was a brisk walk past the bank, greengrocers, dairy, fish and chip shop, Mrs Bailey's combined grocery and post office, the pharmacy, and the solicitor's office – the last of these having been rebuilt after an unfriendly Zeppelin dropped a bomb in 1915.

From there, they headed into Chapel Way and along Lower Field Lane, where one of the turnings was Hedge Place, a pretty, tree-lined cul-de-sac. At its far end, just beyond Enid's small cottage, stood Swift House, a large, white stucco-fronted villa with a sizeable front garden.

There was a sentiment among some that the house was much bigger than one might expect of a man in Norman's situation. Not that it was anyone's business. In Sandham-on-Sea, privacy was a right cherished by all. Of course, that didn't stop gossip. After all, the more private a citizen, the more satisfying it was to speculate about what they might be up to.

At the door, Enid turned the key and pushed.

"Hello? Mr West? Are you there?" She turned to Kate and Jane. "Wouldn't it be embarrassing if he answered."

As it was, no answer came, so they entered.

"Let's stick together," said Kate as she closed the door behind them. "Just in case."

"In case of what?" said Enid.

Kate declined to say.

A moment later, they peered into the front parlour with its marble fireplace, upright sofa, matching armchairs, Persian rug, and walnut coffee table. The only thing it lacked was Norman West.

"Lovely paintings," said Jane, referring to four summer-themed oils of butterflies, ladybirds, wildflowers, swooping swallows and so on.

"Cheap copies," said Enid. "Mr West told me he likes nice things, so he buys imitations in London to make the place look nice."

"Interesting," said Jane.

Kate deduced from her niece's tone that the question of cheap imitations had not been established in Jane's mind.

"Let's try the next room," said Enid, heading into the hallway.

A moment later, they entered the middle room, where again, there was no sign of Norman.

Next, their search brought them to an alcove that had once been a large cupboard beneath the stairs. It was now a space for the newly installed telephone – quite something in Sandham, where Kate was among the few private individuals to have one.

"The notepad's blank," said Enid, taking a peek at the jotter by the telephone.

Next came the garden room, which was home to Norman's desk. There was no sign of the usual occupant though.

Unbolting the back door, they stepped outside.

The rear garden looked stunning with an array of blooms in the borders – among them showy spikes of delphiniums and hollyhocks, bushy white roses and pink peonies. Here, they searched behind the larger shrubs at the back and tried the potting shed – without success.

"Back inside then," said Kate, her gaze lifting from the lower windows to the upper.

They were soon climbing Norman's creaky stairs to the landing, which boasted four bedrooms.

"Which is Norman's?" Kate asked.

"I've no idea," said Enid, somewhat righteously, "although I suspect it's the front one."

Kate led them, although she hesitated at the threshold. If Norman West was no longer on the earthly plane, it would most likely be evidenced behind the ajar door, probably six feet or so to her right.

"Just think," she said. "We spend a third of our lives in bed…"

She knocked.

"Mr West? It's Mrs Forbes with Miss Turpin and my niece."

There was no reply, so Kate took a breath, braced herself for a shock, and entered. Her eyes veered away from the obvious spot, taking in a wing-back chair, a dressing table, floral curtains, and a small, tiled fireplace. Then, with a thumping heart, she turned to the four-poster bed.

"He's… not here," she announced with considerable relief.

They tried the other bedrooms, but all were empty – which meant they were soon reconvening by Norman's desk in the garden room.

"Now what?" wondered Enid.

Kate caught sight of herself in the large mirror over the fireplace. The grey strands in her hair had no intention of abandoning their takeover bid, but a few of those extra pounds below had been vanquished thanks to regular walking.

"Perhaps it's time to go through his drawers," she surmised.

"I suppose so," said Enid. "It's very private though, isn't it, a man's desk. Who knows what he might keep."

"Hopefully, a clue to his whereabouts," said Kate.

"Do we know if he ever married?" Jane asked.

"No, he's a confirmed bachelor," said Enid.

Kate pulled open the first of four drawers and sifted through the contents, which were mainly uninteresting papers. The other three drawers were similarly unhelpful.

"I'm not sure where that leaves us," she said.

Just then, someone rapped on the front door knocker.

All turned as one.

"I doubt he'd knock," said Kate.

"Unless he's lost his key," Jane suggested.

They were soon at the door looking out at a tall man with a bushy grey beard, a straw Panama hat and horn-rimmed spectacles. A bright orange tie was visible in the gap at the unbuttoned top of his light raincoat.

"Oh… good morning," he said in an upper-class accent. "I'm looking for Norman West."

"So are we," said Kate. "I'm Mrs Forbes, a friend. Unfortunately, Mr West seems to have vanished."

"Ah, that's bad news. I was hoping to have a word."

"If you have a calling card, I'll leave it on his desk. I'm sure he'll show up at some point."

"No, I'll try again another time. Thank you."

Kate bade him goodbye and closed the door.

"It might be worth compiling a list of those who know him best."

"Just one thing before we do," said Jane.

She went to the telephone and retrieved the blank notepad.

"Yes, there's something here…"

She took a pencil from her shoulder bag and rubbed lightly over the indentations in the paper.

"It says… 'T. D., Mon, 2 o/c, cottage.' If we assume Mon is Monday, he had a two o'clock appointment with T. D. at a cottage."

"That might explain why he's not at home then," said Enid. "Perhaps you could investigate, just to be sure."

"We can't," said Kate. "What if it's a clandestine affair?"

"Norman's a retired gentleman!" said Enid. "He won't be having clandestine affairs."

"Even so, I think we've gone too far as it is."

"It's just a discreet look, Mrs Forbes, to make sure he's alright."

Kate felt like saying no, but perhaps a quick look into it would allow them all to get back to business as usual.

"Very well, just to reassure everyone. Do you know this cottage he's referring to?"

Enid frowned.

"No, but if you work out who T. D. is, you could try there."

"That settles it," said Kate. "This is absolutely none of our business."

A few moments later, at Norman West's front gate, Kate and Jane watched Enid hurry off. She didn't want to leave her sister for too long in case of a lunchtime rush at the tea rooms.

"Well, Jane… what do you make of that?"

"Cheap paintings?"

"Do you think they're not?"

"I'm no expert, but they look pretty good to me."

"Well, no matter," said Kate. "Getting involved in other people's affairs is the last thing we need. Besides, I'm sure

Norman West will explain the whole thing when he eventually turns up."

Three

Situated in Harbour Lane not far from the quayside, Wilson's Auction Rooms was a relatively recent enterprise. Founded in 1919 by Jack Wilson on his return from the War, it had quickly built a solid reputation. Jack's grandfather had originally run the premises as a ship-chandler, serving Sandham's fishing fleet with everything from sail cloth and rope to mops and buckets, but those days were over.

Kate warmed to the number of visitors strolling around Wilson's vast businesslike interior. It was the first of three preview days, although most sale items had yet to arrive from the rotting, crumbling Brand Hall prior to Friday's sale. She also felt for the Brand family, who had fallen foul of death taxes and debt, causing them to auction everything they owned. Having moved to more modest accommodation in Brighton, the Brands were thinking of demolishing the old pile and selling the land.

Something more immediate was troubling Kate though.

Was she being followed?

Certainly, Ernie Melton was acting suspiciously.

If she turned left at the next display table, would he turn right? Possibly not, as a right turn would lead him to the rear exit.

If only, she thought.

"I doubt there's anything worthwhile here," she said, loud enough for Ernie to hear.

"That's not what you thought earlier," said Jane. "What about that Georgian silver candlestick?"

"Jane, keep your voice down. We're being followed."

"Surely not?"

"Yes, do as I do and act normally."

Jane stifled a laugh.

"Righto, Aunt."

"I have my eye on a number of objects," said Kate, conspiratorially. "The thing is to make sure no one suspects."

"Not so easy with Mr Melton monitoring your every move."

At a long display table, Kate picked up an elegant electric lamp with a carved wooden body and a frilly yellow shade. It looked quite new.

Ernie Melton moved alongside her, seemingly interested in a small wooden horse statuette.

"Mr Melton, what a surprise. I had no idea you were here. Have you seen anything you like?"

"Possibly."

Kate looked to her niece, who was now on the other side of the table examining a brass candlestick holder.

Jane smiled at Ernie.

"I bet you've got an experienced eye on one or two things," she said.

Ernie Melton's face lit up.

"Oh yes, Lady Jane, as you rightly say, one or two things. I'm usually quite lucky at auctions."

Kate raised an eyebrow.

"Unlike the poor Brand family, whose possessions will soon be cast to the four winds."

"Oh?" said Ernie. "Don't you mean the four winds and your front parlour?"

"Not necessarily."

Ernie laughed.

"Hiding an intention to bid on something, eh? It'll soon become apparent once the auction starts."

"Perhaps," said Kate. "Then again, perhaps not."

"It's all to do with psychology, Lady Jane," said Ernie, adopting the mantle of an expert. "If I know she's going to bid for something… say, that mirror over there, then I'd take a closer look. And do you know what…?"

Kate smiled. *You'd see your annoying face…?*

"I'd bid for it during the auction," he explained. "Whereas, if we hide our interest, then a bid by Mrs Forbes during the auction would be too late for me to investigate the item properly. Do you see?"

"Fascinating," said Jane.

Kate huffed.

"I'm sure Jane understands basic common sense."

"It's not common sense, it's psychology," Ernie insisted. "Most people don't even know it's spelt with a silent P."

Kate wished Ernie Melton would be silent.

"There are some lovely rugs over there, Mr Melton," Jane advised.

"Are there? Thank you, I'll take a look."

He duly headed off in the direction indicated.

"There's so much to choose from," said Kate, picking up a brass letter rack. "But how much are things really worth? I mean what should I bid?"

No sooner she put it down, a young man with dark-brown wavy hair picked it up and showed it to a blonde woman with a stylish Dutch bob haircut. Both were wearing maroon sweaters.

"Fliss? What do you think?"

"Ooh," she replied.

Kate meanwhile flagged down a porter carrying a tea chest full of objects wrapped in newspaper.

"Is there much more to come?" she asked.

"Tons, Mrs Forbes. You've barely seen a quarter of it."

Stepping back to let him by, Kate bumped into a fellow bargain hunter. She turned immediately with an apology on her lips, but the middle-aged, blond, moustachioed man wearing a stylish charcoal blazer beat her to it.

"Sincere apologies," he uttered in a soft, very slight accent that might have been German.

"My fault entirely," Kate assured him.

"How about some cushions?" Jane suggested. "They've put some out by the front door."

"Yes, although there are some nice-looking items at the back."

She and Jane were soon at the rear of the premises, where some of the larger objects were waiting to be moved into their final positions. In particular, Kate had a liking for a tall, dark corner cabinet.

"What do you think?" she asked.

Jane shrugged. "That you don't have room for it?"

"I might if I move a few things around."

"Aunt, you'd have to move things into the street."

"Hmm…"

"What do you think of him?" said Ernie Melton, appearing unexpectedly at Kate's elbow. "Might be a famous champion."

He was tilting his head towards what looked like a seasoned boxer wedged into a midnight blue suit. He was speaking quietly with an older man, possibly in his fifties, wearing a mustard blazer and sky blue bow-tie.

"I wonder if the older man's his manager?" said Kate.

Ernie Melton shook his head. "More likely the older chap's an upmarket crook while the bruiser's his hired muscle."

"Don't be ridiculous," said Kate, despite Ernie's observation somehow ringing true. "We need to welcome visitors to Sandham, not accuse them of being criminals."

"How about this?" said Jane, studying a small, polished mahogany coffee table.

"Possibly," said Kate.

Aunt and niece waited for Ernie Melton to move on.

"I'm sorry the weather's against us, Jane. We could be doing so much more."

"That's alright, Aunt. It's already blowing over – and I'll be here all week."

Kate felt an inner warmth. It was good to have her niece come to stay. Especially as Jane had been busy in Oxford for the past month working on some dusty Tudor documents for Professor Peregrine Nash.

Just then, an elegant middle-aged woman in a mint green tweed twin set and pearl necklace moved past them to examine some chairs that another porter had just brought in. She asked him about their age in an educated accent.

Kate turned to Jane.

"Who'd have thought the Brands' possessions would attract such interest. I was right about this being an opportunity to acquire something worthwhile."

Her gaze meanwhile followed the woman in the twin set, who was now having a private word with the possibly German chap. He nodded and whispered something in her ear. Were they a husband-and-wife team working together to secure the best items?

"Aunt?" Jane was peering into a large wardrobe. "You could park a car in here. Is this the sort of thing you're looking for?"

"Very funny, Jane. Perhaps we'll stick to the smaller items then."

Reaching the nearest display table, they were joined by an upright man in his early fifties wearing a naval-style blazer. He was discussing the merits of a footstool with his smartly dressed wife.

Jane meanwhile examined an elegant lamp with a slim porcelain body and narrow pale cream shade.

"This is nice."

"It is," said Kate, "but yet again Ernie Melton has a beady eye on us."

She raised her voice.

"Substandard electrical workmanship by the look of it, Jane. I wouldn't be surprised if it burned the buyer's house down."

They moved along to the next table, where a porter was unwrapping a tall vase decorated in the old floral style. Kate wondered – was this the treasure she'd been looking for?

"Jane, we need to separate ourselves from that vase."

"Do we?"

She steered her niece away.

"I don't think Ernie Melton noticed," she said.

"Noticed what?"

"The vase. I'm ready to bid big money on it. Say, up to a pound."

"You're a crafty one, Aunt. No doubt about it."

"Believe me, I'm relieved to have found the one thing I really want… ooh, look at that figurine!"

"Er… you were saying something about a vase?"

"Jane, just over there stands a Roman emperor. Possibly."

"You're right. Julius Caesar, by the look of it."

"Julius Caesar. You don't suppose…"

"Suppose what?"

"That it's a lost Michelangelo?"

"Well… possibly not."

"Do you know, for Caesar, I might go a little higher than a pound."

"It's often the way with a Michelangelo. Where would you put it though?"

"In the parlour. It would look lovely on a shelf in the cabinet."

"It's too tall, Aunt. It won't fit."

"Well, I'll think of something. The main thing is to skilfully avoid alerting anyone that I've spotted something special."

"Something special?" said Colonel Pickering from nearby.

"Oh, nothing," said Kate, smiling demurely at the retired military man. "I'm really no expert."

"Me neither," he said. "Speaking of which, have you seen Norman West hereabouts?"

"Norman West?"

"Yes, he promised to point out a thing or two for me, but he's an hour late."

Kate thought of Enid Turpin's concerns.

"Well, the auction's not till Friday, Colonel. Perhaps you could rearrange your rendezvous."

The colonel huffed and moved on. But Kate was concerned.

"That's a worry, Jane. If Norman was meeting T. D. yesterday, why has he failed to show up today? If he were able, surely he'd have got word to the colonel."

"It does sound odd."

"I know we said we wouldn't get involved, but…"

"But?"

"Norman West really is the sweetest man. Would you mind?"

"I'm right by your side, Aunt. Where do you suggest we start?"

Four

Under a grey, but thankfully brightening sky, Kate and Jane were on the corner of Lower Field Lane and Hedge Place. Enid Turpin had already tried Norman's close neighbours, so the plan was to cast the net a little wider.

"Hopefully, we'll make some progress here," said Kate, setting her sights on a small, whitewashed cottage along the lane. A moment later, she rapped on its faded yellow door.

It took a while before an elderly woman answered.

"Good morning, Mrs Shepton."

"Mrs Forbes? What's happened?"

"Nothing at all. Lady Jane and I were just wondering if you might be able to help regarding Norman West of Hedge Place."

Mrs Shepton squinted at Kate's accomplice.

"Lady Jane! Such a pleasure to meet you again." She curtsied unnecessarily. "How are you? In the pink, I hope?"

Notwithstanding February's stay, a fair number of years had passed since Jane's time as a regular visitor to Sandham, but back then she made a lasting impression as a friendly face and happy volunteer at various community gatherings.

"I'm very well, Mrs Shepton. And if I recall rightly, you make lovely rock cakes."

"Oh, you remember. How good of you. I've got a batch cooling, if you'll wait there…"

While she hurried away, Kate shrugged.

"We might need to speed up our methods, Jane. I don't think Scotland Yard are slowed by rock cakes."

Mrs Shepton swiftly returned with a small brown paper parcel, for which Jane thanked her as she placed it in her bag.

"Now tell me, Lady Jane, are you still living in London? With your father, wasn't it? Berkeley Square in Mayfair? Not far from Piccadilly and the park?"

"Yes, that's right."

"And your brother? Is he still an army man?"

"Yes, he is."

Kate was a little frustrated at their lack of progress. Yes, Jane's father, Robert Scott, the Earl of Oxley, despite having a country seat at Oxley House in Northamptonshire, spent most his time at the family residence in Mayfair, London. And yes, Jane lived there with him when in the capital. And yes, her brother was a major assigned to the Ministry of Defence, which protocol suggested should never be mentioned. But none of this was relevant to their inquiries.

"Yes, so, getting back to Norman West," prompted Kate.

"Is he alright?" asked Mrs Shepton.

"He's gone missing."

"Missing?"

"Yes, he was due to meet someone with the initials T. D. at a cottage before he vanished. Any idea who it might be?"

"T. D.?"

"Yes, T. D. We don't have a name."

"What's the name of the cottage? I might be able to give you directions. I know Sandham quite well."

"So do I, Mrs Shepton, but we don't have the name of the cottage either."

"Well, there's no use in asking for directions then, is there."

Kate puffed out her cheeks.

"No, I don't suppose there is."

"So, you haven't seen Mr West in the past few days?" Jane asked.

"No, sorry. But good luck in finding him. And do call again. I'll be baking scones on Friday."

They promptly withdrew and tried the next house along. This belonged to a married couple, Mr and Mrs Kenney, although the husband was at work.

"Why's he gone missing?" Mrs Kenney asked.

"We don't know," said Kate. "We think he was meeting someone with the initials T. D."

"T. D.?"

"Yes."

"I know what to do."

"Yes, what?"

"Report it to the police."

"They're not interested," said Kate.

"Not interested?"

"No."

"Then neither am I," said Mrs Kenney. "And neither should you be. Your late husband was a judge. He'd have respected people's privacy."

"I assure you we're only…"

But Mrs Kenney waved away any potential explanation.

"People are entitled to privacy. I mean we haven't been taken over by the Bolsheviks, have we?"

Kate smiled as best she could.

"Thanks anyway."

The next neighbour was Horace Fellows, an elderly gentleman wearing a tatty old vest.

"Mr Fellows," said Kate. "How are you?"

"You're not after money, are you?"

"Not at all."

"Only, I've already given generously, if you recall."

"Yes, I remember," said Kate, recalling the quarter of a penny he donated when she called in support of a children's fund seven years earlier. "No, this is about Norman West. He's gone missing."

"Missing? You weren't after his money, were you?"

"No, we weren't after his money. He was due to meet someone with the initials T. D. at a cottage yesterday."

"T. D.?"

"Yes, have you any idea where this cottage might be?"

"Who's T. D.?"

"We don't know."

"Hmm… T. D…"

Mr Fellows pondered the conundrum for ten seconds or so, at which point an idea seemed to form. His mouth opened a little, he raised a finger… but then shook his head.

"Thanks anyway," said Kate.

Next up was Mrs Yelland.

"Norman West? Missing?"

Kate's news had clearly shocked her.

"Yes, he was due to meet someone with the initials T. D. at a cottage."

"T. D…?"

"Yes."

"Tessa Draper?"

Kate was taken aback. An actual suggestion. She knew of Tessa. It had to be a possibility.

Mrs Yelland shook her head.

"I was never sure about her. Are you saying she and Norman are up to no good?"

Kate's eyebrows shot up.

"We most certainly are not!"

Almost an hour later, at the end of the long lane, Kate sighed.

"Fourteen homes, five of the occupants out – no doubt at work. We could try again this evening, I suppose."

Jane shrugged.

"Aren't we overlooking the obvious?"

"How do you mean?"

"Tessa Draper?"

"Ah… yes… an awkward encounter I was hoping we might avoid."

Five

Kate and Jane paused outside the Alhambra Theatre on North Street. Situated opposite the town hall, it was a late-Victorian building that had recently benefitted from a fresh coat of paint.

"This could be embarrassing," said Kate. "Let's just keep things strictly to Norman's plight. No need to delve into anything else."

They entered the foyer to the sound of muffled laughter from the hall. Judging by the posters on display, Hapless Horatio was doing a grand job.

"We're almost full," said middle-aged Tessa Draper from behind the ticket counter, "but we can always squeeze two more in."

"Ah yes, about that," said Kate. "Are you able to take a couple of minutes away from your duties?"

Tessa's smile dropped.

"Why, what's happened?"

Kate lowered her voice.

"It's Norman West. He's gone missing."

"Norman West… yes, I know the man you mean. I can confidently say he hasn't bought a ticket."

"Ah no, I mean he's been missing since yesterday."

"Oh… well, I can assure we check the entire building every night. You'd be surprised how many people drink too much then lose the desire to leave."

"Yes, so… I'm sorry to ask this, but do you know him personally?"

Tessa's eyes widened.

"No, I don't. Were you thinking I did?"

"No, not at all. It's just that he was due to meet someone at a cottage, that's all."

"Then why come to me?"

"Oh… just a guess."

"A guess? I don't like what you're insinuating, Mrs Forbes."

Kate opted for smiles, apologies and a swift tactical withdrawal before any serious damage could be done.

"The police station?" Jane suggested once they had exited.

"Not yet, Jane. There's one other place worth trying."

*

Sandham's public library was Kate's favourite building. It was Jane's too. Situated just a little further up North Street, it was a wonderful place to visit, whether to read, write or simply contemplate. In winter there would be two roaring fires; in summer its enormous sash windows would be fully open. And, of course, the thousands of intriguing titles would keep the most dedicated reader busy for a lifetime.

Indeed, Kate's nemesis, Ernie Melton had taken this up after the War by starting a journey through fiction beginning with 'A'. Ten years on, he wasn't far off reaching 'B'. Naturally, Kate liked to rile him by talking up the merits of books such as 'Tess of the d'Urbervilles', 'Ulysses', and 'Winnie the Pooh'.

They entered to find a dozen or so people scattered amid the bookcases, and Miss Violet Glover looking up from the librarian's desk beside a sign that read 'Silence.'

"Miss Glover, we're here regarding a missing person..."

"I'm sure you're familiar with the crime section, Mrs Forbes."

"No, a real missing person. Norman West. We thought we might ask around – very quietly."

Miss Glover shrugged and got back to her work.

Kate soon spotted a likely candidate in the reference section.

"Just the man."

A moment later, they were exchanging whispered greetings with the elderly Mr Pointer.

"Can I ask you about Norman West?" said Kate, getting to the matter in hand. "He's gone missing."

"Missing?"

"Yes, he was last seen on Sunday afternoon by Ernie Melton."

"Well, I know he sometimes goes off for bit."

"This might be a bit more than a bit."

"We do have a clue," said Jane. "He was due to meet someone with the initials T. D. yesterday at a cottage."

"But not Tessa Draper," said Kate.

"Any idea where this cottage might be?" said Jane.

"No, but… I saw him on Sunday evening. He was by the quayside. I hope nothing peculiar's happened."

"I'm sure it hasn't," said Kate.

Ten minutes and three conversations later, Kate and Jane were back outside, where the weather was clearing up nicely.

"I'm sorry, Jane. I didn't want to drag you into this. Whatever *this* might be."

"It's alright, Aunt. Honestly."

"I wanted us to enjoy a relaxing few days together. And now look at the mess we've got ourselves into."

"I'm sure we'll get to the bottom of it."

"Yes, I suppose so." But then Kate wondered. "The thing is… if the police aren't interested…?"

"Here's an idea then, Aunt. Why don't we tell them what we know? We've learned a thing or two since Miss Turpin spoke to them. We might be able to jolt them into action."

"Good thinking, Jane. Let's give it a try."

*

Until 1902, Sandham-on-Sea's police cottage was exactly that, a cottage by the quayside where Constable Courtney lived with his mother. It worked quite well, assuming Mrs Courtney wasn't entertaining guests while her son questioned a villain.

Then, on the passing of Mrs Hurst, a wealthy childless widow, the police received an inheritance gift – her detached house in Garston Row, just off the High Street – thereby handing the town a dedicated police house.

Thus, the name of Sandham's law enforcement establishment changed from Mrs Courtney's to Mrs Hurst's. It wasn't until after the War, with the construction of a rear extension and two cells, that the townsfolk began to refer to it as the police station.

Entering its front parlour, Kate and Jane gave their update while the doughty Sergeant Jones and affable Constable Harris, son of Winnie at the tea rooms, listened in silence. Harris, of course, had stood upon Kate and Jane's arrival, but Jones remained seated with a morning paper spread on the desk in front of him. It was pinned down by a mug of coffee on one side and a slice of cherry cake on the other.

Having digested Kate's report, the sergeant finally stirred.

"A cottage? Tessa Draper? The quayside?"

"Yes," said Kate, pinning her hopes on his allegiance to the cause of justice.

"Not interested."

"Not interested?" gasped Kate.

"Norman West has gone off for reasons known only to himself – which is entirely his own affair. I've yet to hear anything that would indicate a crime has been committed."

Kate bristled.

"Sergeant, this is a popular destination for visitors and holidaymakers. If we're to show indifference to missing persons…"

"Mrs Forbes, I don't have the manpower to search Sandham from top to bottom. And who's to say this cottage is *in* Sandham?"

"Well, I… do you think it might not be?"

Jones eyed his cake.

"If you come up with anything significant, you can rely on myself and my constables to leap into action. Good day."

Kate led Jane outside where it was safe to pull a face.

"What now?" Jane wondered.

"I'm not sure," said Kate, "but if Sergeant Jones thinks we're giving up, he's mistaken."

Six

Heading down Royal Avenue towards the seafront, Kate appreciated the brightening sky. Of course, it wasn't just meant to be a restful few days. Jane had been a regular visitor between the ages of fourteen and eighteen, when she was at the Roedean School for girls, not far from Sandham. That period ended though when she went up to Somerville College, Oxford, and later took work as a researcher. With their relationship only recently restarting, Kate was worried this current mess might see her niece choose to leave early.

"I'm so sorry about all this, Jane. I just feel somebody needs to look into it."

"That's alright, Aunt. Although, the sergeant could be right. Who's to say the cottage is local?"

"Yes… he has a point."

With a visit to the Promenade Tea Rooms in mind, they began to cross the street. Kate had decided that a fortifying cup of tea would revive their capabilities. It was also possible that Winnie and Enid had come up with fresh theories.

Before they reached the middle though, a green Sunbeam two-seater car came speeding from the direction of the seafront and hurtled past them.

"The maroon people!" Kate declared.

Indeed, the pair in maroon sweaters gave a cheery backwards wave as if any damage to Kate and Jane would have been of the friendliest kind.

"Ah, young people having fun," said a dark-haired middle-aged man in a pale blue summer blazer. He had crossed the street just moments before. "I'm sure they mean no harm."

Kate smiled at the stranger – no doubt another valued visitor.

"It's quite rare," she reassured him. "On the whole, Sandham is much safer than Brighton."

"Absolutely! Stefano Passoni, at your service. I'm staying at the Crown Hotel, where the hospitality is second to none."

Kate enjoyed his good manners, and the fact that his wholly English accent and undeniably Italian name conjured up an interesting story.

"I'm Mrs Kate Forbes and this is my niece, Lady Jane Scott. I do hope you enjoy your stay, Mr Passoni."

"I'm sure I will."

He nodded politely and set off in the opposite direction.

"The tea rooms then," said Kate.

"You handle visitors well, Aunt."

"I try to help where I can, although I suspect Mr Passoni is a seasoned traveller."

She was keen to see visitors enjoy themselves. She wanted them to return home and spread the word. In her view, it was vital for Sandham to rise above its entry in Bradshaw's guidebook: 'a modest coastal town with a harbour, beach, picture house and theatre. The small public garden has a bench.'

"Have you thought of taking on an official role?" Jane asked.

"How do you mean?"

"Next time there's a vacancy on the council, you could stand."

"Me?"

"Why not? You've got a good grasp of what the town needs. I'd imagine there's no shortage of stick-in-the-mud types on the council who resent change. You'd be a breath of fresh air."

Kate wondered about that. A year on from Henry's passing, she was beginning to reach for new diversions. She would never replace life with her husband, of course, but was Jane right about seeking election at some point? It seemed a leap.

That said…

"Stuffy stick-in-the-muds… there are one or two who've been on the council for thirty-odd years. I remember them opposing the Regal Picture House. They said it would corrupt the town's youth. Henry said if we didn't open a picture house, our youth would move to Brighton."

She fondly recalled being there with him at its grand opening in 1918. The film was 'Tom Jones', a comedy based on the Henry Fielding novel. Ten years had passed since then – far too quickly in Kate's opinion.

"Sandham has charm," said Jane. "Someone needs to work with that, to make it a place people love to visit."

"You're right, but this terrible business…"

Kate came to a halt. Jane stopped beside her.

"Aunt? Are you alright?"

"No-one's seen Norman. Not a single sighting. And yet he left his house. I don't expect people to be at their windows the whole time, but for no one to catch sight of him?"

"Well, we could apply some logic to the situation. It's possible nobody saw him leave. It's also possible he never left the house."

"The police searched it from top to bottom."

"Then perhaps there's another possibility. That he left the house a different way."

"Oh… that's a thought."

"What's at the back of Swift House?"

"Let me think… I'm sure if you head left, you'd soon be back to Lower Field Lane a little way on from Hedge Place. If you were to go straight ahead… that would take you to Stepp Lane, but there's not much there apart from cow pasture stretching a mile or two."

"And if you were to head right?"

"You'd have some woods to get through, but you'd pop out where Stepp Lane arcs round and reaches a dead end. That last bit's called Cliff Way. There must be half a dozen cottages along there. Oh…"

"Well now, Aunt. I'm assuming you don't fancy going back to Swift House and traipsing through the woods."

"Definitely not – but if we head for the cliff end of the promenade, there's a path."

Seven

The coastal path to the east of the town rose quickly from East Avenue to run parallel with the cliffs fifty feet above the sea. Across the water lay France and the Continent of Europe. At its narrowest, by Dover in Kent, the Channel crossing was just over twenty miles. Here, off the Sussex coast, it was more like seventy.

"That's a welcome sight," said Jane. She was pointing out to sea at a distant break in the clouds.

"Ah sunshine… just the thing," said Kate. It wasn't much but she could make out a boat beneath it, no doubt crewed by those enjoying the sudden warmth and the knowledge of a storm having passed.

Up ahead, to their left, before the path's highest point, a branch track led away from the cliff edge to half a dozen cottages set well back along a lengthy stretch. While rear windows and small back gardens faced south to the sea, their front doors faced onto Cliff Way.

"Let's hope we're not embarrassed," said Kate.

The first garden had a potting shed behind a low fence, while two chairs by the back door gave a clear view of the sea and the public path, the latter of which Kate wasn't envious. The thought of having to wave endlessly to friendly passers-by, or worse, ignore them…

"That's Mr and Mrs Hughes' place," she said. "Mr Hughes works at the bank, so he's not likely to be in."

She led Jane along the side of the dwelling, down a dank footpath, and round to a pale green front door facing the deserted road. Here, a sign on the wall stated 'Gull Cottage'.

Kate knocked.

A moment later, a woman in her fifties opened the door.

Kate beamed at her.

"Mrs Hughes, how are you?"

"I'm well enough, thank you. It's Mrs…?"

"Forbes. It seems no time at all since we last sat together in St Matthew's."

"Four months by my reckoning. You usually sit with others."

"Yes, well, I try to sit with a variety of…"

"How can I help?"

"Right, yes, to get straight to the point, we're looking for Norman West."

"I hope you don't think he's here."

"No, of course not. The thing is he's gone missing."

"Missing?"

"Yes, he was due to meet someone at a cottage yesterday, possibly up this way. I don't suppose you saw him pass by either at the front or the back?"

"I've got better things to do than stand at the window watching who passes by."

"I'm sure you have. But might you have seen him?"

"It was all raincoats yesterday. Hard to see who's who. Sorry I can't be of help."

Kate and Jane smiled, thanked her, and withdrew.

Staying on Cliff Way, they soon arrived at the next cottage, 'Cliffside', where retired couple, Mr and Mrs Frost were somewhat put out by news of Norman's disappearance.

"That's a worry, isn't it," said Mr Frost.

"Did you see him pass by at all?" Kate asked. "Most likely, he'd have been wearing a raincoat."

"Not me," said Mr Frost, "Mavis?"

"No, but thanks for bringing it to our attention. If someone's going around making people disappear, we'll keep our doors and windows bolted for the time being."

"I'm not suggesting he's been kidnapped," said Kate, although she was unable to identify the source of her confidence. "Most probably, there's a wholly innocent explanation."

"We look forward to hearing it," said Mr Frost.

The next cottage along looked dilapidated. Its front door was thirty feet from the road along a mossy path.

Thanks to tall, overgrown shrubs, the entrance wasn't immediately overlooked, making it a good place for private meetings.

"Sea View Cottage," said Jane, reading the weathered sign on the gate. "It looks a lot older than the others."

"Most of these went up in the 1860s, 1870s, but long before that there was a cowherd's cottage. I remember Henry's father telling after-dinner tales of smuggling during the Napoleonic era and a clifftop den of iniquity. I think it's this one."

"It certainly looks ancient," said Jane. "It also looks deserted."

They pushed down the path to the front door, where they paused.

"He's with T. D.," Kate reminded them both.

She attempted to rap twice on the central knocker, but one rap was enough to nudge the door open a little.

Aunt and niece exchanged a glance.

"A broken lock," said Jane. "Looks like a single kick was enough."

Kate called tentatively through the crack.

"Hello? Mr West?"

Several seconds of silence followed while Kate took in an odour of damp, which failed to surprise her.

"Hello?" she called again. "Is anyone home?"

She pushed the door open. There were muddy boot prints on the bare boards. Had someone come in via the woods?

"Mr West? It's Kate Forbes. Are you there?"

Jane meanwhile stepped through a gap in the privet hedge to get to the main front window.

"Ah… it looks like someone's had a fall, Aunt."

Kate hurried inside, where, in the front parlour by the fireplace, she came across the fallen individual.

"Oh my…"

Jane joined her – although they were too late to assist in any way.

"Poor chap," said Jane.

It was clear that someone had gone through the sole cabinet's drawers, tipping out the contents – but it seemed to be nothing but rubbish.

"Bumped his head, by the look of it," said Kate. "I wonder how?"

Jane gently nudged her aunt's elbow and drew her attention to a bloodied iron poker on the floor by the window.

"Ohh," gasped Kate.

"At least we know why he went missing," said Jane. "Poor Norman."

But Kate could only shake her head.

"No, Jane… that's not Norman."

Eight

At the police station's front desk, both Sergeant Jones and Constable Harris fixed Kate with a disbelieving stare. So disconcerted were they that Jones even put his mug down.

"Murder?" he questioned. "Are you sure?"

"Yes, I'm perfectly sure."

"Well, that's not good for visitors. They'll all switch to Brighton."

"Are you alright, Mrs Forbes?" asked Constable Harris. "Would you like a seat?"

"No thank you, Daniel. One of you must come right away. I've left Jane guarding the body."

"I'm sure she's safe," said Jones. "Assuming he's dead, like you say."

"He is."

Kate was of course used to events involving the police. Her late husband, Henry, had been a judge who often recounted courtroom tales across the dinner table. And then there had been the business at Linton Hall.

Jones sniffed. “Any idea who he is? Or was?”

“No, I’ve never seen him before. I don’t think he’s local.”

“I’d better get my coat then. Harris, send a boy to rouse Constable Edmonds, then get him to meet me at…?”

“Sea View Cottage on Cliff Way. We got up there by the cliff path off East Avenue.”

“Righto, Harris, Sea View Cottage. Best rouse Dr Howard too.”

“Yes, sarge,” said Harris before turning to Kate. “I’m sorry you and Lady Jane had to come across such a thing.”

“Thank you, Daniel. We’ll be fine.”

“I dunno,” said the sergeant. “A crime wave’s the last thing we need. Did you know there was a break-in at the Crown Hotel yesterday? Some nut turned over a room and had a crack at the safe. Madness.”

He was soon hurrying along the High Street towards East Avenue with Kate doing her best to keep up with him.

“Mrs Forbes, what were you doing at this cottage in the first place?”

“We were looking for Norman West. If you recall, Miss Turpin reported him missing.”

“Yes, well, now we know why he’s gone missing. He’s killed someone and run off.”

“To be clear, sergeant, all we know is that Norman West was due to meet someone called T. D. at a cottage.”

"Yes, and now he's killed this T. D. and run off. Did you see or hear anyone leaving the vicinity?"

"No, but I don't think the crime was committed anywhere near the time we arrived."

"Oh?"

Near the end of East Avenue, just before it met with the promenade, they took the coastal path up to the cliffs. From there, the view across the sea was improving. For a moment, Kate felt pleased for the town's visitors. But now there had been an incident that might have them all fleeing for home.

Unfortunately, it wasn't Sandham's first murder. Back in 1852, when the railway arrived, visitor numbers increased. With a healthy climate, an accessible beach, and a picturesque natural harbour, some chose to move to the town permanently. And yes, in 1865, there was a murder – at the quayside. A drunken fight over a woman, or possibly money.

By 1880, the narrow, higgledy-piggledy Georgian era High Street was extended. Italianate terraces and smart villas went up. A new school opened, as did a library, a town hall and two extra pubs. And yes, a property fraud led to murder.

By the turn of the century, the journey from small fishing settlement to seaside resort was under way. Today, it simply required those in authority to understand that the job was an ongoing one. But murder, it seemed, was no respecter of progress.

As soon as they arrived at the cottage, Sergeant Jones sent Kate and Jane to wait in the back room while he checked the crime scene.

"Dr Howard's on his way," Kate advised her niece.

Jane nodded but seemed elsewhere in her thoughts.

"It brings it all back, doesn't it."

Kate gave an understanding smile.

"Yes, it does. I suppose we never know what lies ahead, but I'd hoped we'd put this kind of thing behind us."

Before Jane could respond, Sergeant Jones came in.

"Just as you described it, Mrs Forbes. This happened a good few hours ago. We'll need a statement, of course, but just tell me again – you came looking for Norman West because he was due to meet someone called T. D. Have I got that right?"

"Yes, the note we found said to meet at a cottage. It took a bit of work to narrow it down to this one. Whether the dead man is T. D. though…"

Ten minutes later, young Constable Edmonds arrived with the balding Dr John Howard, a cheery sort in his late fifties. He'd been good friends with Kate's late husband while his wife, Ginny was a good friend of Kate's.

"John, how are you?"

"I'm well, Kate, but what a shock for you and Lady Jane. I trust the sergeant has made you a strong cup of tea?"

Sergeant Jones turned to Edmonds, who set off for the kitchen. The doctor meanwhile went into the parlour.

Edmonds soon returned.

"Sorry, there's nothing to make tea with. No kettle, cups, or tea."

"Strange household," said the sergeant. "Any idea who lives here?"

"No, sarge. I think it's been empty awhile."

"We'll make some inquiries with the neighbours then. See what they know."

Dr Howard returned without delay.

"The victim's been dead for around twenty-four hours. I can't be more specific than that. The cause of death was a couple of blows to the head with the poker. One to the left side, one to the back."

"A fight?" Jones ventured.

"Most probably, yes. The first blow must have dazed the poor chap. The second one finished him off."

"A nasty business," said Jones. "No doubt a burglary that turned ugly – not that there was much to steal by the look of it. I'd say our top priority is to locate Norman West."

"Yes," said Kate. "He might have witnessed the incident."

"Mrs Forbes, he's more than likely our killer. That said, we won't be able to do much about it if we don't find him."

"Just because he's gone missing doesn't mean he's responsible," said Kate. "He might be hiding from the killer."

Sergeant Jones shook his head.

"Take it from me, Norman West isn't as *missing* as he'd like us to believe. He'll no doubt turn up at some point, bright as a new penny, saying hello, has anything interesting happened while I was away? Now get down to the police station and report to Constable Harris. I'd like full statements as soon as possible."

A few minutes later, Kate and Jane were on the coastal path heading back to town.

"I think Norman could be in danger," said Kate.

"Unless he's the killer," said Jane.

"I know him well enough. He's not the type."

"Sergeant Jones seems to have made his mind up."

"Yes, to be fair, it can't be a coincidence that Norman was due to meet someone at a cottage and now we have a dead man."

"Well, as you say, Aunt, you know Norman. If he's innocent, then someone dangerous is currently on the loose."

"That's a job for the police, of course."

"It is, although we promised Miss Turpin we'd look for Norman. Is that still our intention?"

"I don't know about you, Jane, but I'm worn out. Let's give our statements to Daniel Harris and then have a good rest. After that, we'll see."

Nine

Built in 1888, the Crown Hotel stood on the western corner of Royal Avenue and the Promenade. It was by far Sandham's largest and tallest building, dwarfing all those around it. Sandham's second largest structure, the town hall, was only a third of its size. Designed in the French Renaissance Revival style, which many of London's top hotels had adopted, the Crown boasted six storeys, seventy rooms and two lifts.

For many years it was known chiefly for its first week of opening, when the Earl of Edenfield thought his wife, Lady Edenfield was there enjoying a holiday with her cousin Eleanor. Scandal and divorce followed when Eleanor turned out to be the Prince of Schwarzenberg.

Some forty years on from the scandal, Kate and Jane entered the Crown's oak-panelled lobby – a cavernous space that declared its grandeur without apology thanks to a panelled wood ceiling, a wide oak staircase, crystal chandeliers, gilt-framed mirrors, and oil paintings of various royals.

"Ladies, ladies," greeted a smart young waiter, all too eager to help with their coats. "After I pop these in the cloakroom, I'll smuggle you a free snifter. After what you've been through, it's the least I can do."

"That's very kind," said Jane.

She looked dazzling in a claret evening dress, while Kate's appearance was one of refinement in a dusty pink two-piece.

No sooner the waiter had gone, a tired-looking Sally Inskip at the reception desk beckoned them over in a conspiratorial manner.

"I heard about what happened." Sally's normally sparkling eyes had dulled while her coiffed blonde hair seemed flatter somehow. "It must have been quite a shock."

"It was," both Kate and Jane confirmed.

Sally eyed Lady Jane.

"Have you told your father?"

"Yes, I telephoned him. To say the least, he's very concerned."

"I don't doubt it."

"He advised us to step back and let the police deal with it."

"Ginny and Pru gave me the same advice," said Kate, referring to her friends, Ginny Howard and Lady Davenport.

Sally leaned closer. "On that score, could I ask you not to spread word of it among the guests. No need to spoil their holidays."

Kate puffed out her cheeks.

"The last thing we want to do is talk about it."

"Of course not. Mind you, it's bound to get worse. Danny Harris tipped me the wink that the chief constable has called in Scotland Yard. Their man's due here tomorrow morning."

"Well, hopefully, his investigation will be discreet."

"Discreet? Not if Sergeant Jones is involved. I had him here today asking questions. What you might not have heard is the man you found at that cottage was a guest here."

"Really?" said Kate, genuinely surprised.

"He booked in on Monday then went out. Never came back."

"Poor man," said Jane.

"That's not the only thing. Jonesy's asked me to keep it quiet, so this mustn't go any further…"

Kate leaned in close.

"Trust us, it won't."

"The guest you discovered… his name was William Benson."

"That's odd," said Jane. "Apparently, Norman was meeting someone with the initials T. D."

"Well, anyway, someone broke into his room last night. Turned the place over. Belongings all over the floor, and the mattress too, *and* the drawers all tipped out. Terrible. Obviously, they were looking for something. And not happy with that, they had a go at the hotel safe. Not that they took anything. That's to say, there wasn't anything worth taking."

"The sergeant mentioned the room and the safe earlier. Poor you, Sally. You've had quite a time of it."

"That wasn't the worst of it."

"No?"

"Ah," said Jane. "I'd imagine the police needed someone to identify the body."

Sally's mood darkened.

"Not a pleasant experience, I can tell you."

"Well, let's hope that's an end to it," said Kate. "Scotland Yard's man will ask you questions, no doubt, but things should soon return to normal."

"Let's hope so," said Sally. "But, for now, not in front of the guests…?"

"Absolutely," said Kate.

But her gaze was now elsewhere, on a man emerging from the salon on route to the dining room. It was the man with the beard, straw hat and spectacles who had called at Swift House earlier. Moreover, his mood seemed pensive, possibly worried even.

"Perhaps an aperitif in the salon?" Jane suggested.

"Yes," said Kate, "I think we've earned it."

*

The Crown's spacious salon was quiet, with just a few patrons dotted about here and there. One of them, crusty Colonel Pickering, had fought in a long-forgotten war – at least it would have been long-forgotten but for him talking about it at the drop of a hat. Kate nodded to him and steered Jane in the opposite direction.

Here she spotted the maroon people in a corner, although now they sported matching dark green attire. They seemed preoccupied with each other to the point that Kate felt obliged to look elsewhere.

Seated beside the fireplace was the man with the faint German accent Kate had bumped into at Wilson's. He was alone, reading a newspaper, although he looked up and smiled at the new arrivals. Kate and Jane smiled back. At Wilson's, he'd been in cahoots with his classy wife. No doubt he was waiting for her now.

"How about over there?" said Kate, indicating a couple of padded stools either side of a small table by one of the large windows.

Jane signalled to the waiter.

"Two dry sherries, please."

"Coming right up."

"Well," said Kate, thudding down onto a seat. "What a day. I'm exhausted, shattered, worn out… but I doubt I'll sleep. It's as if my veins have been plugged into an electric socket."

"It's adrenalin," said Jane. "The way to ease it is to take exercise."

"Now, let's not resort to drastic measures, Jane."

Kate noted her niece's smile and attempted to suppress her own, without success. When Spanish Flu took Jane's mother, Annette, nine years ago, Kate had searched for ways to help her niece in any way she could. Annette had been Kate's younger sister, so the desire to be the best aunt possible was never far from her thoughts.

"How about a long walk tomorrow, Aunt. The weather's improving."

"Yes, why not. Fresh air, wonderful views… I suppose we should forget the other business."

"It's probably for the best."

"Yes, although… poor Norman. I do hope he's not outside somewhere."

The waiter beamed at them.

"Two dry sherries."

"Ah, just the thing," said Kate.

The waiter placed their drinks on the table before them, and a bill on a small dish beside Kate's glass. The bill stated: 'No charge.'

She thanked him while Jane raised her glass.

"To happier times, Aunt."

Kate raised her own. "And sunnier days."

Both took a sip.

"Mmm," murmured Kate as the warmth of the sherry reached the back of her throat.

While they enjoyed their drinks, they discussed the weather more fully, and then the prospects for Sandham's growing holiday trade boosting local businesses over the coming months. After that, Kate steered them onto Friday's auction at Wilson's.

"I really don't have space for much," she said. "Perhaps I'll restrict myself to one small item."

"The vase or Julius Caesar?" questioned Jane. "Or perhaps the full-size dining table I saw you admiring?"

"Speaking of the auction," said Kate in a lowered voice. "Wasn't he there this morning?"

She was indicating a man wearing a charcoal grey blazer and crimson bow-tie entering the salon alone.

Jane glanced over.

"Yes, he was with a man we felt might be a boxer."

"That's right. I thought he might be the boxer's manager, but Ernie Melton suggested he might be a crook and the boxer his hired thug."

"Anything's possible," said Jane, "but I noticed him looking over the more expensive items at Wilson's. He might just feel the need to have a protective friend."

The man in question ordered a drink at the bar and then looked around the salon.

"Ladies," he called by way of a friendly greeting. "Are you guests?"

"No," said Kate. "We live locally."

"Ah, I'm just down from London. Thought I might find something at this auction you're holding. Clifton's the name. Sir Gerald Clifton."

"Well, good evening to you, Sir Gerald," said Kate. "I'm Mrs Forbes. This is my niece, Lady Jane Scott."

"Names I've heard before," he said.

Kate was surprised.

"May I ask where?"

"In the hotel lobby earlier. A most unfortunate business."

Kate cringed. So much for keeping it from the guests. The gossip machine never ceased, apparently.

"Yes, most unfortunate," she concurred. "Will you stay on?"

"Yes, of course I'll stay on. Things happen. I'm only sorry to hear you ladies had to contend with it. I'll be here till Friday come what may."

"Has anything taken your fancy at the auction rooms?" Kate asked. She was keen to move on.

"One or two items. I'd best not say though. Don't want to start a bidding war. How about you? Do locals bid?"

"Yes, I have my eye on one or two things. As you say though, it's not wise to reveal too much."

Kate didn't mind paying the right price, but judging by Sir Gerald's fine clothing, items such as the vase might fly high over her one-pound target should he get involved.

"That poor chap today," he said. "A friend of yours?"

Kate's heart sank.

"No, he was a visitor to the area, we think. We were only there looking for a local man who's gone missing."

"Oh, sounds like an intrigue."

"Not really. Well, at least we hope not. He's bound to turn up soon enough."

"Has he been missing long?"

"Most likely since Monday."

"Hopefully, he wasn't out in that dreadful weather. He'll have holed up somewhere, no doubt. Trouble at home can send a man off and away. Perhaps it's just that."

"No, Norman lives alone. His disappearance is a complete mystery."

"I see… well… you've got me worried about him now. Please do reassure me all's well when you find him."

Ten

Ten minutes had passed in which the ladies ordered another sherry and Sir Gerald became ensnared by Colonel Pickering at the bar with a tale relating to past heroic endeavours.

"Well, here we are, Jane. A nice dinner to look forward to at the end of a terrible day. Once Scotland Yard's man has spoken to us, we'll hopefully be able to enjoy a quiet few days together."

Jane smiled.

"A quiet few days is exactly what we need."

"Mrs Forbes! Lady Jane!"

The call from the Englishman with the Italian name had an engaging tone. He also looked dapper in a green blazer with an open necked cream silk shirt.

"Mr Passoni," said Kate.

"Mind if I join you?"

"Oh, er… not at all."

He did so, pulling up a stool by their table.

"Thanks. And, please, it's Stefano."

"Well then, Stefano, have you had an enjoyable day?"

"I have. But I heard some distressing news. You poor ladies."

Once again, Kate's heart sank a little. This wasn't the thing she wanted to dwell on.

"Yes, well, the police should get to the bottom of it soon enough and we can all move on. Ah look, the waiter. Perhaps he can get you something."

As Stefano ordered a gin sling, a stylish middle-aged couple came into the salon. The man looked smart in a navy-blue blazer, white silk shirt and golden yellow cravat, while his partner wore a beautiful black satin evening dress. Kate recognised them from Wilson's.

"Good evening," she called over to them.

"Good evening," the man replied. He and his companion duly came closer to Kate and Jane's table.

"Did we see you earlier?" the man asked. "At the auction house?"

"Yes, we were there. Just a mild interest, nothing more. I'm Mrs Kate Forbes and this is my niece, Lady Jane Scott. Sandham is my home. Jane's visiting me for a few days."

"A pleasure to make your acquaintance. I'm Peter Langham. This is my sister, Beatrice Fry. We're here for the auction. With any luck, we'll leave on Friday with something worthwhile."

Kate introduced them to Stefano Passoni. If he were a lone visitor, he might benefit from getting to know fellow guests.

"Well, here's to the weather," she said, raising her glass once the introductions were over and their drinks had been ordered. "It seems to be picking up."

"Yes, indeed," said Peter. "We came in by yacht on Sunday, which wasn't too bad. Thankfully, we had Helios safely in the harbour for Monday afternoon. It was quite a storm."

"It wasn't so good this morning either," said Kate, thinking back to the gales. "I wouldn't like to be at sea in bad weather."

"Very wise," said Beatrice.

"A yacht sounds exciting," said Jane. "Do you sail Helios far?"

"Not often enough," said Peter.

"It's usually just across the channel to France and back," said Beatrice. "Occasionally, if the seas are *extremely* calm, we'll go around Spain and Portugal to the Mediterranean, but I don't like to be caught in the big swells."

"For me, it makes the perfect year," said Peter. "The summer months in Monte Carlo, the winter months in the Alps – just like my grandfather chose to live."

"The Alps?" said the man by the fire. "It's where I'm from. I'm Swiss. Max Drexler."

"Do you ski?" Peter asked him.

"Yes, but not recently. These days I live in Geneva. It's not skiing country."

"Peter's fascinated by skiing," said Beatrice.

"They ski all winter in the north of Italy," said Stefano, "but city people usually stay out of it."

"But I hear it's catching on," said Peter. "Expensive resorts and all that."

"Yes," said Max, "there are a few now. A strange sight perhaps to see grown men wobbling on their skis. Where I'm originally from, we would either ski from childhood or not bother at all."

"I should like to learn," said Peter.

Kate found it both fascinating and odd that anyone would pay to travel somewhere freezing cold and then risk life and limb.

"How interesting," said Sir Gerald, having freed himself from the colonel. "I love to hear about other countries."

"Do you travel yourself?" Beatrice asked him.

"I have a soft spot for Paris, but I'm really no traveller. It's all too much of a fuss."

"Jane's visited a few places," said Kate.

"Not that many," said Jane. "But yes, Vienna, Rome and Athens. And I've visited Egypt to see the Pyramids."

"How fascinating," said Beatrice. "I'd love to see the Pyramids. All that history…"

"And a growing trade in antiquities, I hear," said Peter.

"Plundering might be the word," said Jane.

"My niece is an archaeologist," Kate explained.

"Well, she has a point," said Peter. "Once important historical artefacts are smuggled away, they tend to be sold to the highest bidder and never seen again."

"It's true," said Jane. "Since Carter's discovery of Tutankhamun's tomb, there's been something of a frenzy."

"But don't forget the curse," said Peter. "Carter's patron, the Earl of Carnarvon, dropped dead during the excavation."

"Peter, really," said Beatrice.

"Sorry. One small whisky and I'm forgetting the day you poor ladies have endured."

"No need to apologise," said Kate. "I'm sure Jane doesn't believe in curses. She's disturbed enough ancient remains to wake a whole army of vengeance."

"We should talk about pleasant things," said Beatrice. "Is there a concert hall in Sandham?"

"Yes, a small one," said Kate. "The Royal Gala Hall. It was named after the Prince of Wales who was due to open it in 1889, although he was unable to come. We kept the name though; the sign had already been painted. The old place is in need of restoration now, but last year we had some wonderful piano recitals – Chopin, Schubert, Mozart…"

"I do admire Mozart," said Beatrice. "Especially his operas. Have you heard his work sung in German?"

"Er, no."

"We were at the opera in Vienna recently for a selection of arias. We had seats near the president."

"Italian opera's the best," said Stefano. "Mozart said so. You must try La Scala in Milan. I've been a few times myself. Everything performed there is perfection."

"You're a champion for Italy," said Kate, "just as I'm a champion for Sandham-on-Sea."

"Yes, it's true I'm proud of my Italian heritage, although I've lived in many cities over the years: Paris, Amsterdam, Berlin, Milan, London…"

Over the next ten minutes or so, Peter and Beatrice moved closer to Sir Gerald by the bar, while Stefano was drawn into a conversation with Max Drexler.

It was then that a woman entered the salon clothed in a beautiful emerald-green evening dress. Yet again, this was someone Kate recognised from Wilson's. She smiled at the new arrival – who returned the smile and looked set to take the stool Stefano had vacated.

"Do you mind if I sit here?"

"Not at all," said Kate. "Welcome to Sandham-on-Sea."

"Thank you."

Once the waiter had attended to her, Kate continued.

"Are you enjoying your stay?"

"Thank you, yes. I'm glad the weather's improved."

"Oh, absolutely. By the by, I'm Mrs Kate Forbes and this is my niece, Lady Jane Scott."

The woman's eyes lit up, but just for a second or so.

"Miss Teresa Alvaro."

"Oh wonderful. An Englishwoman with a lovely Spanish name. How interesting. Are you here with anyone?"

"No, it's just me. I came down from London this morning."

"Oh right," said Kate with a smile she hoped covered her puzzlement. After all, didn't Miss Alvaro have Mr Drexler whispering softly in her ear at Wilson's?

"As for my name – yes, I was born in Madrid but schooled in England from the age of four. James Allen's Girls' School, Cheltenham Ladies' College and St Hilda's, Oxford. My mother insisted on it."

"Wonderful. And now you're living in London?"

"Yes, St John's Wood. Do you know it?"

"A little, yes."

The conviviality continued for a while longer until Kate's rumbling stomach insisted it was time to make a move to the dining hall.

"That was interesting," said Jane as they left the salon. "Mr Langham talking about artefacts being smuggled."

"From Egypt, you mean?"

"Yes, but it made me think of closer to home. Sea View Cottage may have had smuggling connections."

"Possibly, or it could just be old stories."

"Many stories have a grain of truth, Aunt. What if it's true? What if there's a smuggler's hidey-hole there? And what if it's big enough to hide a man?"

Kate stopped dead.

"Are you saying…?"

"Yes – what if Norman West was there all along and never left?"

To Kate, it seemed preposterous, and yet strangely difficult to dismiss outright.

"Should we tell Sergeant Jones?" she wondered. "Or take a look first?"

Eleven

In Cobb Lane, Wednesday morning sunshine lit up the face of a detached, red brick Victorian house and the lobelia-lined path that led to a burgundy front door with twin frosted glass panes set into the upper half. Parked down one side was Gertie – a 1926 cherry red two-seater Austin Seven Chummy with a mischievous liking for playing dead on cold mornings.

To Kate, it was home. To Jane – a home from home.

In the dining room, on upholstered seats at a large oval table, they were finishing off a breakfast of soft-boiled eggs, toast and coffee. There had also been much chewing over the business that lie ahead.

"It's not quite a holiday, is it," Kate mused.

"Of course it is," insisted Jane. "Obviously, getting involved in murder and mystery isn't what you'd put on a 'Things to do in Sandham' brochure, but… actually, that would draw in thousands. Ten of thousands, even. All we'd need do is recruit them to help us find Norman."

"Perhaps you've already found him, Jane."

Since leaving the hotel salon the night before, the notion that Norman West might not have left Sea View Cottage had intrigued them. While neither fully believed it, both were eager to put it to the test.

According to Jane, the morning's newspapers featured stories based on the Chief Constable's public statement. While not naming Sea View Cottage, the name of Norman West cropped up as a person of interest. Kate though had avoided reading any of it in her copy of *The Times.*

Around nine o'clock, they were ready to set out – Jane in a cream and orange striped summer dress, Kate in a green floral day dress with her trusty light grey cardigan. Both were wearing sensible shoes.

Leaving the house, Kate glanced up at the sun playing peek-a-boo with a few cotton-wool clouds in a blue sky. It was the perfect day – almost.

"This business – it's bad for Sandham."

"It is," said Jane, "but these things eventually fade from the public's thoughts."

"Only if the perpetrators are caught."

"True, although whoever killed Mr Benson is still in town, so there's a chance."

"Yes, a hotel break-in after the murder does suggest it's an ongoing matter. I just hope nothing sinister happens before Scotland Yard swoop."

They made their way along the High Street to East Avenue. It wasn't long before they reached the path up to the cliffs. Here, Kate paused.

"We *are* doing the right thing, aren't we, Jane? I mean we're definitely not investigating a murder. We're simply looking for a missing friend. I wouldn't want Sergeant Jones or your father to get the wrong idea."

"Dad's fine. And he trusts you. As for the sergeant..."

"Yes, well, we're looking for Norman West then. That's all."

"That's all," agreed Jane. "There's no law against searching for a missing person. And it's not interfering with a police investigation if finding him reveals what happened at Sea View Cottage."

They began their march up the path.

"To think people are here to enjoy themselves, Jane. All this worry is the last thing they need."

"It's good to see you getting involved in the town's affairs, Aunt."

"I wouldn't put it quite like that. I just feel we could do more to attract visitors. I'm actually onto the vicar at the moment. You never know, but we might soon have a wonderful historical attraction at the church."

"You never mentioned it."

"I was hoping to surprise you. The thing is... I want visitors to tell everyone about their trip to Sandham-on-Sea."

"Oh, they'll be doing that all right."

"Jane… please."

"Sorry, Aunt. That was flippant." She reached out and squeezed her aunt's hand. "Have you given any more thought to making things official? I was serious about the town council. You're well known, and you have a good name. Uncle's reputation won't do you any harm either. He's fondly remembered and his standing as a judge is the sort of thing councils like to associate themselves with."

"I'm only the widow of a judge."

"Even better. You'd have more time to devote to improving Sandham."

"Yes, well… I get the feeling 'improving' might be seen as 'interfering' by some."

"I'm sure you'd enjoy the challenge. And if you ever become mayor, you could banish Ernie Melton to Brighton."

"Don't tempt me."

At the top of the cliff path, before it branched off to the cottages, they paused to take in the view.

"The sea looks calm," said Kate. "Perfect for pleasure boats. We should have more of them visit Sandham Harbour."

"Perhaps the Harbour Board could do more to attract them. I wonder who could push for that?"

"You're determined to get me on the council, aren't you."

"You'd certainly breathe some life into it."

"It's true we're held back by stuck-in-the-mud members, but right now there's something going on that's doing far more damage to our reputation."

A few minutes later, on the branch path that led to the cottages, Kate shared an idea.

"I did wonder about improving the gardens at the end of the promenade. What do you think?"

"I think… we're being followed."

"Pardon?"

"Someone's following us."

"Are you sure?"

"Yes."

"Alright, but let's not turn around suddenly. It could be an innocent holidaymaker. We don't want to frighten them."

"We won't. It's the boxer."

Twelve

Kate wondered what to do. They were walking slower and slower.

"When did you first catch sight of him?"

"When we turned off the street onto the path. I didn't suspect anything at the time, but when we stopped to look out to sea, he did likewise. Only, from his vantage point by the thorn bushes, there isn't much of a view."

"And now he's decided it might be interesting to take the branch path to the cottages. Any normal visitor would continue along the cliff path to the highest point. That's the best view you'll get."

"If we don't stop and turn, we might have to confront him down the side of Sea View Cottage."

"Yes, much better to say hello here, Jane."

They stopped and turned – and were faced with the smiling boxer approaching from thirty feet away. He was dressed in a thick, dark blue suit and heavy black brogues, which put some distance between him and the concept of a holidaying hiker.

"Morning ladies," he called. "I was looking for the best view out to sea."

"Back to the cliff path and follow it upwards," said Kate. "The views are wonderful. After that, I'd suggest going back the way you came, along the promenade and up to the lighthouse. You'll get a whole new aspect from there."

He touched the edge of his trilby and turned. The ladies waited until he was well away before resuming their own journey.

Kate wondered. "Why do we think he was following us?"

"Hard to say. He has some kind of relationship with Sir Gerald Clifton. Hired muscle, according to Ernie Melton."

"No doubt Sir Gerald sent him to keep an eye on us. He knows we were looking for Norman when we discovered Mr Benson. Actually, do you think the boxer could be the killer?"

"Possibly," said Jane, "although there's nothing to link him to the crime."

"True. And of course we're not investigating a murder. We're merely trying to find Norman."

"Exactly. If we *were* investigating the murder, we'd be trying to discover what the boxer was up to on Monday."

"Jane, this whole business needs a speedy resolution."

"I agree. The sooner we can enjoy a relaxing clotted cream tea, the better."

At the rear of Sea View Cottage, they peered over the fence. All seemed quiet.

"A smuggler's cottage, Aunt?"

"Possibly."

They went round to the front where the curtains were closed and the busted door was shut, thanks to a piece of card wedged between it and the frame.

Kate's skin prickled.

"I don't suppose there was much point in posting a constable here all night."

She pushed. The card fell to the ground and the door swung open.

Despite the deathly quiet atmosphere, they paused to listen. Kate then gave a little shrug and called out.

"Norman? Are you hiding? It's not the police, it's Kate Forbes."

There was no reply.

"Let's search, Jane."

Beginning by the front door, they moved along the narrow hallway, tapping the walls and stamping on the floorboards. This brought them past the bottom of the stairs on their right and to the parlour on their left.

Here they stopped.

"The crime scene," said Jane.

"Indeed."

"What if we find him?"

"We'll hand him in. And if we don't find him, we'll have narrowed our search."

They entered the parlour.

"I don't know him, Aunt, but he doesn't sound like a killer. If he had a role in that poor man's death, I'd imagine it being peripheral."

"Do you really think Norman could be here?"

"It was just an idea."

"And, as usual, a good one. I'd bet a bottle of untaxed brandy there's a hidey-hole somewhere."

"Do you think it still goes on? Smuggling, I mean."

"It may do. If the stories are true, they would have sent a rowing boat out to meet a bigger boat, then hurried back to the beach. From there, it's up the path to the top and back here. Much safer than using the harbour."

"So, let's imagine ourselves a hundred years ago… we've just met a French boat off the coast, and we've rowed back carrying a few crates of brandy. Now what?"

"Well, first and foremost, we're delighted to have French brandy at the tax-free price. The thing is, where do we hide it?"

Jane considered it. "I'd want to hide the stuff as quickly as possible. I'd also want quick and easy access to it if I'm to split the load later."

She looked around the room.

"A fight that ended with a dead man."

"Yes."

"Over what?"

"No idea."

Kate looked to her niece who was pulling up the edge of the rug.

"Moth-eaten thing," she said as she dragged it aside.

"At least it's something," said Kate. "Think of the draft blowing up through the gaps. It must be freezing during the winter."

"Yes… although… look closer. Isn't that a trap door?"

Kate peered at the floor, looking for a square or a rectangle. There wasn't one. But…

"Oh, is that…?"

"It's been cut with alternating long and short edges so it doesn't immediately stand out."

Jane placed a finger in a knot hole and pulled.

Beneath was a small chamber, just large enough for a curled-up man to hide for a short while.

"Empty," she said. "Unless you include a dead spider."

She pushed the trap door back into place and put the rug back.

"Now what?" said Kate.

Jane dusted her hands.

"We should try the other rooms."

"And if he's not here?"

"Then we'll need a new plan."

Thirteen

At the gate to Cliffside, Jane thrust her hands into her coat pockets. Kate smiled sympathetically.

"I know it's a slog, Jane."

"No, it's fine. I'm just getting tired of asking innocent people questions that worry them."

"We could leave it to the police."

"No, we need to find out what we can."

"Don't worry, we'll keep it short. Besides, Mr and Mrs Frost seem pretty robust."

She knocked at the door.

A moment later, they heard a heavy bolt sliding back.

"Sensible," Kate whispered.

Then two more bolts slid back.

Finally, Kate was able to say hello once again.

"Mr and Mrs Frost, we're sorry to bother you a second time. We just have a couple of things to ask."

"Sergeant Jones visited yesterday," said Mr Frost. "We're still in shock."

"I can imagine."

Kate felt for them. This whole business would prove unnerving to the toughest of souls.

"That poor man," said Mrs Frost. "I know it's none of our business, but who was he and what was he doing there? And who was he in league with, and who did he annoy enough to get himself killed? And how does Norman West fit into it?"

Mr Frost folded his arms.

"We couldn't help the police, Mrs Forbes, so I don't see how we can help you."

"I understand entirely, but is there any little snippet of information you've dismissed? It might be something that seems inconsequential, but we'd still be very glad to hear it."

"No, sorry… but frankly, shouldn't everyone be looking for the killer? Unless you're suggesting Mr West is the killer?"

"We're not suggesting anything of the sort."

"We asked Sergeant Jones the same question, but he started talking about the amount of work he has on his plate."

"Yes, well, Norman West was meeting William Benson. That's all we know. Most likely, when Norman arrived, Mr Benson was already dead. No doubt Norman didn't fancy hanging around to find out who killed him."

Mrs Frost raised an eyebrow.

"Unless the killer chased Norman, caught him and killed him too. He might have tipped the body over the cliff!"

Kate wanted to smile in a way that might reassure them, but it was hard to know which face muscles to pull.

"In these situations, there's usually a surplus of theories," she ventured.

"That's true. It's possible Norman was the target but the killer got the other chap by mistake. Or Norman and the killer were working together to get Mr Benson…"

Kate held up a hand to halt the speculation.

"We were wondering about a man who looks like a former boxer. You know the sort of thing. A rearranged face. Might you have seen someone like that on Monday?"

"No," said Mr Frost. "Do you think he's the killer?"

"Probably not," said Kate. "The main thing is finding Mr West. That would certainly answer a few questions. Now, please help us if you can. We were wondering who owns Sea View Cottage."

"It's Mrs Digby. I expect you know her."

"Alice Digby? With the white hair and bad leg?"

"That's her," said Mrs Frost. "She used to live there, but now she rents it to someone and lives with her daughter."

"Do you know who she rents it to?"

"No, sorry."

"There doesn't seem to be anyone living there," said Jane.

"No, well, I don't think they've moved in yet."

Kate's brow furrowed.

"Isn't Mrs Digby's daughter Yvonne Vincent?"

"That's right," said Mr Frost.

"Doesn't she live by the quayside?"

"Right again. You should be a detective."

Kate smiled. It was hard to tell whether she had just been paid a compliment.

Next, they tried Gull Cottage.

"Mrs Hughes, how are you?"

"Shocked. Utterly shocked. My husband's shocked too. And the lady in the bakery – she's shocked. And Mr Hart in the greengrocer's…"

"Right, yes, I'll get straight to the point. We're still looking for Norman West."

"And he's still not here."

"No, of course not. But have you seen or heard anything since yesterday?"

"I told Sergeant Jones everything I know. The whole thing's a terrible business, but I've nothing to add."

"There's a man who looks like a former boxer. Have you seen him around?"

"No, I haven't. Unless you mean the one who was following you when you came up a while ago."

"Yes, that's him. He wasn't around on Monday, was he?"

"I'm not sure, but if I were you, I'd be careful."

"Sound advice. Thank you.

Kate and Jane tried the three dwellings the other side of Sea View Cottage. Here, they interviewed for the first time Mr Thompson at Channel View Cottage, Mr Rushton at Highpoint, and Mr and Mrs Cross at a cottage with no name. In each case, the result was the same. They had already told the police everything they knew and had nothing further to add.

"Well," sighed Kate at the end of it all. "Mrs Digby then."

Fourteen

A tight huddle of 18th and early 19th century buildings in narrow lanes dominated the area around the quayside. It was here that Sandham and the harbour met – originally providing homes, workplaces and services for fishermen, boatbuilders, sailmakers and all manner of trades associated with seafaring.

Just off the quayside, along from Mrs Dobson's Superior Dining Rooms and the Prince of Wales pub, Kate and Jane arrived at Alice Digby's daughter's house in Quay Place – a pale blue cottage with a white front door and small windows. A sign gave its name as 'The Captain's Rest', no doubt referring to an important local figure in Sandham around 1850, when it was built.

As for the current owners, Kate didn't know much about Mr and Mrs Vincent, beyond an understanding that the husband was a merchant navy man who was often away at sea.

As it was, Alice Digby answered the knock at the door. She was a small, silver-haired woman in her mid-sixties with a welcoming smile and a limp that required a walking stick.

"Hello, how can I help?"

"Mrs Digby," said Kate, "you may know me, Kate Forbes. This is my niece, Lady Jane Scott."

"Yes, of course. I'm guessing this is about the unfortunate business at Sea View Cottage. We've had the police here and your names were mentioned. It must have been awful."

"It was," said Kate. "We were quite shaken by it."

"You have my sympathy. My daughter and I were shaken by having Sergeant Jones asking questions. Really, what a to-do."

"Yes, the sergeant can be somewhat direct, but he means well."

"He just came out with it – there's a dead man at Sea View Cottage; what can you tell me about it?"

"Yes, I suspect he missed the Chief Constable's bulletin on using tact. The thing is, Jane and I were there looking for Norman West. He's a friend who's gone missing."

"Norman West, yes, the sergeant said he'd vanished into thin air. It's a worry, isn't it."

"Mrs Digby," said Jane, "would you mind me asking you something?"

"No, of course not, Lady Jane. A pleasure."

"You lived at Sea View Cottage."

"Yes, up until a couple of months ago."

"And now you're now renting it to someone?"

"Yes, Reginald Unsworth. He's a businessman. Something to do with machinery. Mind you, he hasn't moved in yet. He had to go off abroad."

"Do we know where?"

"Belgium, I think."

"Belgium?" questioned Kate. "Aren't you concerned he might not return?"

"Not really. He paid a year's rent in advance."

Kate was surprised.

"Didn't you find it odd for him to pay all that money and then go abroad?"

"No, not at all. He said he needed a base where he could come and go as he pleased. He's due back in a couple of weeks. You'll be able to ask him all about it yourselves."

"That's very helpful," said Kate.

"We told all this to the police though. I mean I'd prefer to not go through it all again."

"Let me assure you, we're merely…" But before Kate could finish, Mrs Digby's daughter, Yvonne Vincent, appeared at the door.

"Mrs Forbes? Please don't think I'm being rude, but what's your interest in all this?"

"Mrs Vincent, hello. We're just trying to find Norman West. That's all."

"Isn't that a job for the police?"

"Yes, of course, but before we discovered the unfortunate chap at the cottage, we were asked by a friend of Norman's if we might look for him. At that point, the police weren't interested. That's why we were there."

"That doesn't make sense. Why go there at all?"

Kate raised an eyebrow.

"We found a note. Norman was due to meet someone."

"At Sea View Cottage?"

"The note didn't specify. We simply arrived there as part of our search."

"I see… well… like Mum says, it's been empty a while now. She lived there with Dad until he passed away. It's been difficult for her."

"Of course, I understand. I lost my own husband last year."

Alice and Kate shared a moment that only they could fully understand.

"This Mr Unsworth," said Kate. "What do you know about him?"

"He seems a trustworthy type," said Alice. "You know the sort: mid-forties, tall, a former army officer who's gone into business. I'm thinking now someone knew he was abroad and thought there might be valuables at the cottage. The thing is, it's quite old and needs some work doing before he can move in properly. He said he'd sort that out when he gets back."

"Well, he'll have a shock when he learns what's happened."

"No doubt."

Kate and Jane thanked Mrs Digby and her daughter, then headed to the nearby quayside.

"I'm more worried than ever about Norman," said Kate. "Something tells me things are much worse than we think."

On the quayside's stone cobbles, they took in a busy scene. A fishing boat had landed a catch. Notwithstanding interest from the local fishmonger, the chef of the Crown Hotel, and a number of seagulls, most of the catch would soon be on the railway bound for London's Billingsgate Fish Market.

"Morning, ladies," said Ned Dawson, a seventy-year-old pipe smoker sitting on a pile of empty crates away from the action.

"Morning, Ned," said Kate. "I'm sure you remember my niece."

"I do. Good to see you again, Lady Jane."

"Good to see you too, Ned.

"Always a good sight, that," he said, indicating the unloading activity.

"It is," said Jane, "although I suspect it was a lot busier in the old days."

Ned's eyes sparkled at those magic words.

"Hake," he said.

Both Kate and Jane knew not to interrupt.

"Plaice, turbot, sole… When I was a boy, we had a hundred boats and four hundred and fifty fishermen. Now look at it. Seven boats and thirty men."

Kate nodded. Local fishermen were struggling to compete with the east coast fleets fishing the more profitable North Sea.

"Flounder, gurnard, herring, mullet, whiting…" Ned continued.

"I'm sorry to change the subject," said Kate, "but we're looking for Norman West."

Ned shrugged. "Don't really know him. A new arrival, by the sound of it."

"The thing is he's gone missing."

"Yes, so I heard."

"You have?"

"We had the police asking questions. Young Constable Edmonds. He was here about twenty minutes ago. I was sorry to hear you got caught up in that business at Sea View Cottage."

"Yes, we were sorry too."

"You know old Charlie Hicks?"

"Yes?"

"Working on a boat, he is. A new paint job. Lovely navy-blue body and white edging. Very smart."

Kate glanced at her watch.

"Well, we won't keep you, Ned."

"Charlie reckoned it ought to have a thin line of red too. Bring out the white, he reckons."

"Yes, well…"

"While we were discussing paint, a boat came in with a French crew. That man who was killed…? Charlie and me reckon he got off this boat. The crew didn't hang around for him though. Storm warning."

Kate was suddenly glad they hadn't left.

"Was this Monday morning?" Jane asked.

"Yep."

"You're sure it was the same man?"

"The porter from the Crown Hotel was down here this morning. I described the bloke who got off the boat and he agreed – it was the same man who booked into the hotel soon after I saw him."

"Did you tell Constable Edmonds any of this?"

"No, he left when I started talking about paint."

"Well, thank you, Ned. As usual, you've been most helpful."

"Thirsty work, all this talking."

Kate handed him a few coins.

Ned touched the edge of his cap.

"So," said Kate, "Norman was meeting a man who came in from France."

"How about we try Swift House again," said Jane. "There might be something we overlooked yesterday."

"Good idea. We'll go via the Promenade Tea Rooms and get the key from Enid."

Fifteen

At the end of Hedge Place, Kate and Jane stood once again outside Swift House, with its sizeable front garden. And once again, Kate reminded herself that it was none of her business that a retired department store worker should have such a large home.

With little confidence of finding Norman, but at least some hope of discovering an overlooked clue, she opened the front door. Immediately, she could hear someone in the back room.

She turned to Jane.

"Norman? Or the killer looking for him?"

Holding the door half-open and ready to pull it shut again, she called out.

"Hello? Is somebody there?"

"Who is it?" a young woman responded.

Kate wondered. Was this T. D.? She pushed the door wide open as Tilly Crawford, a local cleaner, came out from the back into the passage.

"Mrs Forbes?"

"Tilly… T. C…?"

"Sorry?"

"Is Mr West home?"

"No, and what's more, someone's broken in."

"What?"

"They smashed the glass in the back door. You'd better come in. Hello, Lady Jane. It's nice to see you again."

"Hello, Tilly. I'm sorry you've had such a shock."

"It's nothing like the one you and Mrs Forbes had yesterday."

All three went into the front parlour where a degree of upheaval was evident.

"I came in to do my weekly clean. It's two hours every Wednesday – not that he makes much mess. But today, in all the rooms… well, there's drawers turned out, cupboards and cabinets searched, all sorts of mess. I've telephoned the police. Sergeant Jones is busy dealing with something else first, but he'll be along as soon as possible."

Kate shook her head.

"We've been looking for Norman since yesterday. We've still no idea where he is."

"I've heard the stories," said Tilly. "And, of course, his bed hasn't been slept in. You don't think he killed that bloke then ran off, do you?"

"We're hopeful he didn't," said Kate, "but it's more important than ever we find him. Now, he had no way to leave Sandham except on foot. And the weather was bad. That said, if he was working with the killer… then, yes, they might have fled in the killer's car. But that doesn't explain these break-ins. The hotel and now here. It's more likely the killer's looking for something in Sandham."

Tilly shuddered.

"The killer was here…?"

"Long gone, I'm sure," said Kate.

"Mind you," said Tilly, "whoever they were, I don't think they took anything. At least not as far as I can see."

"I expect you know this place pretty well," said Jane.

"I do. I've been cleaning for Mr West since he came to Sandham. I know the house very well."

"Is it possible the thief took some small objects?"

"No, I don't think so. Anyway, none of Mr West's stuff is worth much."

Kate shrugged.

"Perhaps you were wrong, Jane. If this lot was valuable, some of it would have gone, for certain."

"True," said Jane. "Unless the thief was looking for something specific."

Tilly frowned.

"Are you sure Mr West couldn't leave Sandham? Only sometimes he visits his sister in London. He's devoted to her, you know. The thing is – he always tells me and Miss Turpin when he's going so we don't worry."

"What's the sister's name?"

"I don't know, sorry. He always refers to her as his sister. That's it."

"I wonder if there's an address?"

"There'll be one in his little green book."

She picked it up from the floor and handed it to Jane, who flicked through the first few pages.

"This won't be much use."

She handed it to Kate.

Despite there being plenty of addresses and telephone numbers, there was a problem.

"How odd. All the entries are in initials. And as for the addresses, they make no sense."

"W for West," said Tilly. "Unless she's married."

Kate checked.

"Right, we have three entries under W."

She took the book to the telephone and dialled the operator. A moment later, she gave a London number and waited while it rang.

"Sloane 2123," said a woman's voice. "How can I help?"

"Oh hello, I'm trying to get in touch with E. West."

"I'm sorry, there's no one with that name here."

"Is there anyone there with the initials E. W…?"

"No, sorry."

Kate apologised and ended the call.

"Are you sure you don't know his sister's details?"

Tilly shook her head. "No, sorry."

"You've never been here when she visits?"

"She never visits. Mr West says she doesn't like travelling. Something to do with her knee."

"One down, two to go then," said Kate. "Perhaps you'd like to try, Jane?"

Over the next few minutes, Jane got through to the other two W entries – J. W. and R. W. – both without success.

"What a strange address book," Kate declared.

They continued their search in the garden room where Norman's desk stood by the window. Nearby, the glass in the back door had been smashed to gain access to the sliding bolt. Consequently, there was a sharp, jagged mess on the mat beneath it.

"The safe!" cried Kate. A painting had been tossed aside to reveal a safe built into the wall. The door was open. The contents were gone.

"It's alright," said Tilly. "He doesn't keep anything valuable in there. I checked his money. That's all fine."

"He hides his money elsewhere?"

"Yes, I'd better not say where."

"Tilly, Mr West has vanished and could be in mortal danger. This is no time for secrecy."

"The biscuit tin has a false bottom. He keeps it there. I had to check, but it hasn't been touched. Just as well – it's over a hundred pounds."

Kate's eyes widened.

"That's a fortune."

Tilly nodded. "It's what my husband earns in a year for fifty hours a week in the ironmonger's."

"Probably best hand it to Sergeant Jones," advised Jane.

"Yes, and speaking of which, he said not to touch anything."

"Quite right too."

"There could be a clue among this lot," said Kate, referring to a scattering of documents below an open drawer in the sideboard.

"It's just old papers," said Tilly.

But before any thought could be given to donning gloves, there was a knock at the door.

"I'll see who it is," said Tilly as she hurried off.

"I'd imagine we're about to be thrown out," said Kate.

A moment later, Sergeant Jones could be heard in the hall.

"Right, Edmonds, search the house. Start at the top. And I do mean the top."

"The loft space, sarge?"

"We want to make sure he's definitely not at home."

Kate and Jane came out from the garden room, causing the sergeant's frown to deepen.

"You two…"

"We were just leaving," said Kate.

Outside, heading up the front path, Jane said what they were both thinking.

"This isn't going well, is it."

"No, it's not. Perhaps it's time we reported our findings to the police."

"Aunt Kate, I don't know if you noticed, but Sergeant Jones isn't interested in our efforts."

"I'm referring to young Daniel Harris. If it helps him get one up on Sergeant Jones, so be it. Besides, we might learn when Scotland Yard's man is due."

*

Arriving at the police station, Kate peered in through the bay window. Constable Harris was seated behind the desk. Spotting them, he waved and came to the door.

"Good morning, ladies. How can I help?"

Kate smiled.

"Hello, Daniel. Sergeant Jones has made it abundantly clear that we mustn't hinder policework, but we have some information regarding Norman West."

"You've found him?"

"No, but we feel there's more we could all do. I include the police in that."

"Sorry, Mrs Forbes. You're not to get involved."

"In looking for Norman West? It's a citizen's duty to help those in need, including people who are lost."

"Norman West is linked to a murder."

"We know – we found the body."

"Yes, but you're to steer clear of the investigation. I hope that's plain enough for you."

"As plain as can be, Daniel, but it's already in the newspapers. The whole of England will have read about Mr Benson's demise over their porridge."

"I really must warn you off, Mrs Forbes. I'm a police officer."

"Yes, a police officer I used to say oochy-coochy to. Now, we've heard a rumour that Scotland Yard are sending someone down. Is there any news on that?"

"Yes," said a voice from the back room. "I've arrived."

A moment later, Inspector Leonard Ridley appeared in the doorway.

"Oochy-coochy, indeed…"

"Inspector! It's you!" exclaimed Kate.

"I'm glad to see your powers of observation haven't deserted you, Mrs Forbes."

Greetings were then exchanged between Ridley and the two ladies.

"Well," said Kate, "you certainly got here fast."

"Ah well, I didn't have to travel far. A colleague of mine's recuperating at the police rehabilitation home in Hove. He came off a motorcycle a couple of months back. I was just seeing how he's getting on."

"Oh, inspector, your poor colleague. Is he on the mend?"

"Another month and he'll be back to light duties. Perhaps not motorcycling though. But enough about police matters. Why are you here?"

"Hold on a moment, inspector. Let's look at you. Have you lost weight? A good diet is vital for effective police work."

Ridley looked down at himself.

"I'm the same as ever, thank you."

Kate beheld him. Grey-haired, in his early forties, standing tall in an everyday dark grey suit. And that voice – confident but never strident. An experienced detective and a credit to the working-class background he may or may not have come from.

"We're looking for a missing friend, inspector."

"Yes, I've been brought up to date regarding your involvement. I'm sorry you found yourselves involved in such a brutal business, but it's for the best that you stay out of it."

"We will, but before we go, we must tell you about Mr Benson. It seems he arrived on a French boat before booking into the Crown Hotel. Separate to that, Jane and I were followed this morning by a chap who looks like a former boxer. We believe he works for Sir Gerald Clifton. At least, they were together yesterday at Wilson's Auction Rooms. They could be looking for Norman West."

"I'll look into it."

"Thank you. I'd just say we don't believe Norman's the killer, which – if Jane and I were investigating – would mean viewing the boxer as a suspect."

"Mrs Forbes, as you say, you're not investigating."

"No, we're not."

But Ridley sighed and turned to Constable Harris.

"This boxer. Is it someone we know?"

"No sir, but I'll look into it."

"Right," said Ridley. "I have a telephone call to make. Please stay out of trouble."

"Yes, inspector. Remember though, I know Norman better than you and your colleagues do. I have an insight into the man. I know the way his mind works. Please don't throw that away."

Ridley considered it.

"Alright then, carry on looking for him – but any sniff of danger, back off and report to me."

Sixteen

Deciding on a light lunch, Kate and Jane headed for the Promenade Tea Rooms in search of a cheese and tomato sandwich. As they reached the door, however, they were faced with Stefano Passoni leaving.

"Ladies," he beamed. "A pleasure."

They nodded and entered.

"Such an interesting man," said Winnie, her eyes following Mr Passoni as he crossed the street to the Crown Hotel. "He bought everyone a cake and told us all about Europe. The mountains with snow on them, the lakes, the sights in Milan, Paris and Amsterdam, the food, the wine, the cheese…"

"Did he ask about Norman West?" asked Jane.

"Oh… well, yes, he did. He wondered if anyone knew where Norman might be. Oh, it was lovely to talk about pleasant things. It helps take the mind of that other matter.

And on that score, did you know Scotland Yard's man is here? They sent Inspector Riddle."

"It's Ridley," said Kate. "Jane and I have met him before."

"You don't mean…?"

"Yes, at Linton Hall. He'll soon sort things out."

"I do hope so," said Winnie. "Honestly, I wish Enid had never asked you to get involved."

Ernie Melton looked up from his *Daily Mirror*.

"It's in all the newspapers," he said with a hint of excitement.

"No need to read any of it out," said Kate.

"*Brutal murder in Sandham-on-Sea*," Ernie read aloud. "*A visitor to the coastal town was killed with a poker*."

"Yes, that's enough, thank you."

"*Police have little to go on at this time. The name of the dead man has yet to be confirmed*."

"Ernie, please…"

"I haven't got to the good bit yet. *The body was discovered by Lady Jane Scott, daughter of the Earl of Oxley. Lady Jane is known to be a friend of Norman West, a man the police wish to question in connection with the murder. At this time, Mr West is missing from his home in Sandham*."

Jane looked a little shaken. But Ernie was grinning.

"No mention of you, Mrs Forbes."

Kate waved it away. "Anyone who wants to get their name in the newspaper must have a screw loose."

"Too true," said Winnie. "One day you're this, the next day you're that. You have no say in how they write about you. I'm happy staying out of the national newspapers."

Ernie scoffed. "You'll never get in the papers. Not unless you poison someone." He glanced down at his cup of tea.

"On more important matters," said Kate, turning to Winnie. "Could we have two cheese and tomato sandwiches, please."

But Winnie was preoccupied.

"It's funny how everyone's interested in Norman. That man out there… he was asking about him earlier."

Kate and Jane turned to the window just in time to see a bearded man walking past. Sunlight glinted off his spectacles.

"Curious," said Jane.

"Of course, we know the truth about Norman now," said Winnie.

"Do we?" said Kate.

"He's having an affair with Tessa Draper. That's why he's hiding."

"What?" said Kate. "No, that's not right at all."

"It is – it's the reason he's gone missing."

Kate and Jane shared a glance. It was clear they had inadvertently started the rumour. But Kate wasn't having it.

"Winnie, that's just a silly bit of gossip."

"Are you sure?"

"I'm absolutely certain."

"I wonder what fool started it?"

Just then, a young man got off a Norton CS1 motorcycle by the door and came in.

"Colin Nelson," he said loudly – not because Winnie might be hard of hearing but for the benefit of all. "I'm a reporter with the Sussex Chronicle."

There was an audible muttering.

"How can I help?" said Ernie Melton.

"I'm looking for Lady Jane Scott. Any idea where I might find her?"

Kate sent death rays directly at Ernie causing him to falter.

"Er… yes… um…"

"I've tried the police," said Nelson, "but they just repeated the official statement. What I'm after is the story from the human angle."

"I can give you one or two details," said Ernie. "I know the psychology of the lady in question. She and Mrs Kate Forbes, widow of a judge, were up the cliffs for a picnic when they required water."

Kate's brain tried and failed to get a grip on Ernie's description, but she supposed getting a grip on his neck instead wouldn't be the wisest way to deal with it.

Meanwhile, Ernie continued. "Their friend Norman West was a regular visitor to a nearby cottage where he was having an affair with—"

"Ernest Melton!" yelled Kate. "You're doing Sandham a disservice."

But Ernie shrugged and continued while the reporter carried on jotting it down.

"…and then they found a body. And they're shouting, 'Oh no, not Norman!' and then they're going, 'oh, hang on, that's not Norman!' and then their psychological state of mind was anxiety and… er, despair. My name's Melton, by the way. M-E-L-T…"

"Ernie, you weren't there!" insisted Kate.

"On the subject of crime," said Winnie, "there was a break in at the hotel. Someone went through one of the rooms. They also got into the hotel safe. Must've been looking for something. According to Sally at the hotel, the room had been booked by William Benson, but he never came back."

"He was the one who ended up dead at the cottage," said Ernie.

"I was getting to that," said Winnie. "Mr Benson came in on Monday, booked a hotel room, went up to the cottage and was killed. The question is why? And by who?"

"That's two questions," said Ernie.

Colin Nelson tapped his teeth with his pencil. "We're up to date regarding Mr Benson, but I want a bit more. Anything you might have heard…"

Kate tilted her head towards the door and Jane didn't require any extra encouragement to leave. A moment later, they were outside.

"We'll eat a bit later," said Kate, squinting a little against the brightness of the day.

"This is getting out of hand," said Jane.

Kate winced. Wasn't she meant to be Jane's responsible older companion?

"Let's stroll, shall we?" she suggested.

They took to the promenade.

"I'm sorry about all this, Jane. Of course, I'll speak to your father. I'll explain it's all my fault."

"Don't be silly, Aunt. We were trying to help someone. He understands that."

"That was before your name appeared in the papers. He won't like that."

"He trusts you. That's never going to change."

Kate gazed across the beach. It had been deserted during the bad weather, but now there were dozens of people enjoying it. Most were under hats or umbrellas, but some had taken to the growing trend of baring as much skin as possible to acquire a tan. Meanwhile, Mr Allegri was setting up his ice cream stand, no doubt anticipating sales.

A squeal!

It gave Kate palpitations, but it was a mother, father and three small children playing in the gentle waves breaking on the shore. Not far from them, a doughty fellow dived in causing Kate to shudder. Sunshine could be a cruel trickster. Water that looked inviting would be cold enough to turn the poor chap blue – although he surfaced and seemed content enough to stay there.

Just then, a party of young couples came onto the beach.

"Looks like fun," said Kate. "There's nothing like good company and a carefree mood."

Jane smiled.

"When I was young, I used to pretend I'd find buried treasure in the sand. I always think of this as a happy place."

"Me too," said Kate.

Jane was right. Children had all the best ideas. Treasure on the beach? Perhaps Sandham itself was a treasure.

She turned to face Royal Avenue. Eastward from the tea rooms, along the sea front, the promenade passed a couple of side streets before it eventually gave way to the cliffs just beyond East Avenue. Westward from the Crown Hotel, the promenade passed a few more side streets before reaching the public gardens and a split in the path – to the right, the harbour, and to the left, a rise to a rocky promontory on which stood the Sandham lighthouse. On the other side of this was the harbour's narrow entrance.

She badly wanted to keep her mind off murder.

A question then. Should she seek to become a town representative? Yes, it was fun to be a self-appointed ambassador using her local knowledge to assist visitors. But to seek a seat on the council? Where would she start? What would her main argument be? Sandham couldn't match Brighton for star names topping the variety bills, but the town could surely do more to attract visitors.

"Do you know what I miss?" said Jane. "Bank Holidays. I haven't been here for one in ages."

"Oh, Bank Holidays… yes…"

On those rare golden days when almost everyone got a day off work, the crowds would flock to the seaside. In Sandham, there would be performers on temporary outdoor stages on the promenade and beach. And what variety! Concert parties with both operatic and popular songs to join in with, hearty comedians to raise the spirits with laughter, Punch and Judy professors, pantomime Pierrots, clowns and jugglers.

Kate sighed.

"We need to sort out this Norman West business."

"Yes, we do."

"He's a good man. A regular church goer. A helpful sort. He's popular with some of the ladies. Speaking of which, we're meant to be having lunch with Pru and Ginny tomorrow." She was referring to a regular weekly lunch at Pru, Lady Davenport's grand house further round the harbour. "This whole thing is getting in the way of… well, everything."

From their vantage point, they watched the reporter get back on his bike and ride away.

"You said Norman's a regular church goer, Aunt. What if he spoke to the vicar in confidence?"

Kate considered it. “Let’s have a word with him, shall we?”

With a purposeful stride, they set off.

“Will I get to see your visitor attraction?” said Jane.

“It’s not quite ready to view,” said Kate, “but yes, we should push a little on that front. Who knows, we might yet put Sandham in the news for all the right reasons.”

Seventeen

From the promenade, Kate and Jane entered Royal Avenue on the Crown Hotel side of the street, where the boxer emerged right in front of them. Rather than acknowledge their presence, he sidestepped them instead on his way to the promenade. Clearly, he had pressing matters in mind – perhaps pertaining to Sir Gerald Clifton, who followed him out of the building.

"Sir Gerald," said Kate. "Good afternoon. Looks like the weather's perked up no end."

"Yes, yes… very pleasant." For a moment, his gaze followed the boxer, but he quickly came to his senses. "I thought I might take the air. A stroll along the front, I think."

"It's just the thing to cheer anyone up." Kate was mindful that Sir Gerald was most likely an innocent man. "And please let me reassure you once again that Sandham is perfectly safe."

He touched the brim of his hat and smiled.

"I'll be on my way."

"The church then," said Jane.

They strolled briskly up Royal Avenue to its junction with the High Street. Here they turned left and crossed over. Passing Garston Row where the police station was sited, and Kate's turning, Cobb Lane, they were bound for the next right turn, Church Lane.

"We should stop a moment," said Jane as they reached the corner.

"A stone in your shoe?"

"No, not a stone. Yesterday, the boxer, and now, Mr Drexler."

"How do you mean?"

"Don't look, but he's following us."

Kate stiffened. "Are you sure?"

"I think so. He's stopped near your turning. If I'm not mistaken, he's looking in the baker's window."

Kate studiously looked the other way, to the harbour end of the High Street, where its straight run met narrower streets that twisted and turned by the quayside. This was home to the drapers, florist, souvenir shop, amusement arcade, ice cream parlour, the newsagent and confectioner, the ladies' hairdresser, the men's barber, a motor garage and many others.

And now? It was a place of intrigue.

That's not what Kate wanted for Sandham.

"Perhaps he's looking for Miss Alvaro," she suggested somewhat optimistically.

Jane raised an eyebrow.

"I doubt she's in the baker's, Aunt."

Kate sighed. There was no point in hoping the problem would go away.

"Right then… he's feigning interest in a shop window. Let's do likewise."

She pretended to be fascinated by the window right in front of her – Kenway's Funeral Directors, where a sign stated, 'Appointments Not Necessary'.

"We might need to act, Aunt."

"Hmm, yes – no point in us all staring at windows for the next hour. Any ideas?"

"We could confront him, but it might prove more awkward for us than him. Why don't we walk up to the church. Something might occur to us."

"I wonder why he's following us though."

"According to the newspapers, I'm a good friend of Norman West's."

"I was trying to pretend that had nothing to do with it, Jane."

"I think we have to accept we're not the only ones looking for Norman."

Kate peered down Church Lane.

"Do you remember St Matthew's Gardens?"

"Yes, of course."

"I'll lure him into a trap."

Church Lane had two distinct halves. The High Street end was lined by some of the largest and smartest houses in Sandham. In contrast, the church end was more natural, with bushes, trees and a bench by a pond opposite the church.

Kate and Jane headed up there and skirted the pond with a hurried, cheery hello to two children throwing stale bread to the ducks. Getting to the bushes was the thing.

"Jane, you hide behind that overgrown laurel, and I'll turn the tables on him."

Kate pressed on and became increasingly aware of someone nearing. She could hear his breathing. Panting, really. Very disturbing. What kind of monster..?

A spaniel came out of the undergrowth and sniffed her leg.

"Shoo!"

Worried she might be spotted, she pushed on further through the trees.

And yes, he was following. No doubt about it. This was no pooch.

She continued to the point where the trees stopped on one side of the cemetery. Here, she crossed the lane and went through the north gate into the other part of the cemetery on the far side of the church.

She turned suddenly.

Yes, it was Max Drexler by the gate, but he turned also.

Kate followed, slowly at first, but increasing her pace. Somehow though, she lost sight of him. Had he ducked behind the wall? She stepped out to confront him.

But it wasn't Drexler. He'd given her the slip. Instead, it was Harold Wootton, the church verger who was noted for taking his minor official position seriously.

"What's going on?" he demanded.

"It's nothing, verger. I was following a man."

"You can't follow men here. It's sacred ground."

"Verger, really."

"Inappropriate activities are not permitted on church property."

"Don't be ridiculous. The man I was following was acting suspiciously. Perhaps you saw him."

"I saw no one. It's called minding my own business. More people should try it."

Resisting the urge to give the verger a verbal volley, Kate huffed and headed off towards the main entrance. It was just a matter of waiting for Jane.

Eighteen

Situated on high ground overlooking both the harbour and the original village, the Church of St Matthew had dominated Sandham-on-Sea since the 12th century. Much to Jane the archaeologist's delight, monks had built it over an earlier Saxon church mentioned in the Domesday Book, with remains of the original building still visible in the lower walls of the nave. The addition of a tower with bells followed in the 14th century, while the new porch and oak doors dated back only three years to 1925.

To Kate, the church had always been Norman in style, but when Jane came to stay in February, her growing expertise brought a new understanding. Norman architecture between the 10th and 12th centuries was Romanesque in style, mainly because the Normans had aspired to build a similar empire to the Romans.

Of course, Kate had noted all this. Perhaps, one day, she'd write it all up in a short guide for visitors. Then again, perhaps not. She wouldn't want to be accused of pushing herself too far.

"There you are, Aunt!"

Kate was relieved to see her niece coming through the lychgate.

"He got away, Jane."

"Yes, I followed him back to the High Street. He headed down Royal Avenue."

"Right, then let's get back to our task."

As Jane joined her, she turned to face the entrance – a wide arched doorway with a depiction in the stonework above it of a man laying palm leaves in front of Jesus on a donkey. In centuries long ago, thousands of Normans would have passed through this doorway. Now, they were seeking just a single Norman.

They entered the airy nave, which was fringed with decorated columns that held up the roof and created a ten-foot wide ambulatory either side of the main space – in which pews either side of a central aisle offered enough hard wooden seating for a hundred parishioners.

Teresa Alvaro was seated there, and Stefano Passoni too, just a few feet away from her.

Interesting, thought Kate.

She looked to the other end where the altar sat in the chancel space. There was no sign of the vicar though.

Following them in was the verger. Perhaps she would put him off with something innocuous.

"We're here to see the vicar," she told him. "I was wondering if he's had any more thoughts about my visitor attraction."

"Not that I'm aware of."

"He may not have discussed it with you."

"All important matters are discussed with me. It's my job to maintain order."

"Verger, this is St Matthew's Church, not Wandsworth Prison."

"Yes, well, if this is to do with the old wall painting, it's beyond repair."

"We don't know that for certain."

"That's my considered opinion."

"It's covered with panelling."

"I was here in 1911 when the panelling was repaired. I saw the patch of wall."

"Really?" said Jane. "Your eyes would have been the first in centuries to do so."

"Well… I suppose so."

Just then, the vicar came in.

"Ah, Mrs Forbes and Lady Jane – always a pleasure to see our champions of historical matters."

"Thank you, vicar," said Kate.

"Good to see you," said Jane. "Aunt Kate's been telling me you're thinking of uncovering an old fresco."

"Ah, yes… as I've explained to Mrs Forbes, it's probably a bit too much of a faff."

Kate wasn't having it.

"Vicar, it's for the good of Sandham. And, who knows, you might put St Matthew's on some kind of pilgrimage trail."

"I very much doubt it."

"I'd love to see it," said Jane. "And I'd be happy to make a donation to the church fund."

"Oh… right. Well, we do have a few repairs that need tackling. Yes, very well, come along tomorrow morning at ten. We'll take a look together. I know someone who can do the heavy work."

"Wonderful, thank you."

The verger shrugged and departed. But Kate signalled to the vicar to dally a moment longer.

"We were wondering about Norman West."

"Yes, poor chap. Missing presumed lost somewhere. I wonder where he is."

"We think he's still in Sandham."

"Oh?"

"He most likely went missing on Monday. The bad weather probably rules out leaving by boat, the police have checked the railway station, and he doesn't have a car or a bicycle. It's unlikely he walked – not with all that storm and tempest."

"No indeed."

"It's possible, of course, that if the killer had a car and was in league with Norman, then he might be far away by now. But break-ins at the hotel and Norman's home suggest the killer is still here in town."

"Well, it's all very intriguing, but I'm not sure what I can do about it."

"Can you cast any light on Norman's frame of mind?"

The vicar considered it.

"He did seem to be a man in search of forgiveness."

"Forgiveness for what?"

"That's between him and you know who."

"Yes, of course."

"It's odd though. You're the third person to ask about him."

"Really?"

"Yes, first there was a chap who I think might have been a boxer."

Kate exchanged a glance with Jane.

"Interesting. Who was the other one?"

"A chap in a blazer and nautical cap."

"I wonder if that's Peter Langham? Would you say he was an upright man, early fifties, perhaps?"

"Yes."

"I reckon it is then."

"Well, the more the merrier," said the vicar. "Hopefully, with everyone getting involved, Norman will soon be found."

Just then, Teresa Alvaro came past on her way out, smiling at them as she did so.

"It's lovely to have visitors coming to the church," said the vicar.

"There's another one over there," said Kate, eyeing Stefano Passoni who had remained seated.

"Yes," said the vicar, "I had a chat with him earlier. He was admiring the church architecture. It turns out we've both visited Notre Dame in Paris. Have you been?"

"No," said Kate, "but did he ask about Norman West?"

"No."

"Or did he mention the lady who just left?"

"No, why do you ask?"

"Oh, no reason, vicar. We'll see you tomorrow at ten."

A few moments later, standing outside, Kate took in a lungful of air and breathed out long and slow.

"I don't know about you, Jane, but I feel like everyone else knows something we don't."

"About Norman, you mean?"

"Yes, and I feel that being polite and pleasant has got us precisely nowhere."

"We could kick some doors in and twist a few arms," Jane suggested.

For a second or two, Kate looked at her niece with a degree of alarm. Then they both laughed.

"Well done, Jane. There's no need for negativity on my part. I'll tell you what there *is* a need for though – getting to the bottom of this whole business."

"It might have been Peter Langham asking the vicar about Norman," said Jane.

"Let's have a fortifying sandwich then… and after that, we'll have a look along the harbour shore. If Peter Langham's there, we'll have a word."

Nineteen

The lighthouse stood on the highest point in Sandham, a hundred feet above the sea, west of the promenade, on the eastern jaw of the harbour entrance. It was a popular destination with a metal railing on the cliff side that was perfect for leaning against whilst looking out to sea. From there, the land sloped down to the harbour shore and its various boathouses, slipways, repair yards and the main quayside before it eventually arced round to meet the River Harley's estuary.

Kate and Jane had already tried the lighthouse, but as expected, its heavy door was locked. And besides, there were visitors milling about during the day, while at night, it was manned. This was no place for Norman to hide.

Coming off the slope brought them down to the harbour shoreline path, which ran just above the myriad of small boats that would float at high tide and be beached at low tide, when it would be necessary for the owner to drag or push a small craft into the water. Currently, the tide was neither in nor out.

Here among visitors strolling and enjoying the sunshine they came across the first harbour-related operation – a shabby boat house with a cracked side window.

"It looks abandoned," said Kate.

She peered in through the window.

"Ah, it's not!"

A man came to the door. Kate didn't know him but thought his name might be Chivers.

"Mr… Chivers?"

"What's your game?"

"Sorry," said Kate. "We're looking for a missing friend. Norman West. Do you know him?"

"I can't think why you don't knock on the door like normal people."

"I'm sorry."

"Well, that's fair enough then. Now, Norman West… he's as good as a mystery to me. If he's gone missing, I doubt I can help you."

"Well… thanks anyway."

"With that body you found and him going missing… it all adds up, don't it?"

"Not necessarily," said Kate.

"It sounds like it all adds up. Shouldn't you be leaving it to the police?"

"We're not replacing the police. We're just trying to track down a missing friend."

"Fair enough. If I hear anything…"

"You'll get in touch?"

"No, I'll inform the police."

The next building along was the sturdy timber-framed boat house and slipway for Guinevere, the town's sea rescue vessel. Local volunteers had operated such a boat for more than a century now, and since 1870 had been members of the Royal National Lifeboat Institute.

Here, crewman Joe Cullen was varnishing the south-facing side of the building where the sun would do most damage. It was a straightforward business to establish with cheery Joe that Norman wasn't there.

Pushing on, they came to Bill Thornton's repair yard. He and his apprentice, Albert, were on the water not too far away in an old four-seater rowing boat – the kind the local rowing club used in races. Kate presumed Bill and the boy might be testing it before working on it.

While it seemed unlikely that Norman would inhabit Bill's establishment, they decided to take a peek anyway. Behind the repair shed, another rowing boat caught their eye – not sleek like the competitive boat, but short and wide and built for leisurely pursuits. It had a heavy tarpaulin over most of it, although the corner nearest them had been pulled back.

"I'm not saying I have a sixth sense, Jane, but…"

While Jane waited, Kate crept up to the boat and peered into the gloom beneath the cover.

A squeal!

A scream!

An elderly cat leapt out and scooted off, leaving Kate breathless and Jane trying to look concerned, but failing.

"Was that Norman?" she asked.

"No… that was not… Norman."

Kate puffed a while longer as she watched the old moggie head off to the next boat house along.

It wasn't long before they followed and arrived at this much larger building – one capable of sheltering two or three small boats. Sitting outside on a battered old chair, Ned Dawson was asleep.

"Sorry to bother you, Ned," prompted Kate.

He jumped awake.

"Oh… afternoon, ladies. Still looking for Norman West?"

"Yes, and with no luck at all," said Kate.

Ned took out his pipe and relit it.

"You won't find him here," he said amid a billow of smoke.

"No, I suppose not. We're just trying to eliminate all the obvious places."

Kate looked across the harbour to Holton, a much smaller settlement than Sandham situated on the other side.

"You gonna try over there?" said Ned.

"I think we should."

"If I remember rightly," said Jane, "it's a half hour walk."

"Ten minutes by rowing boat," said Ned.

"That's what I was thinking," said Kate.

They walked on, all the way to the quayside. It didn't look promising.

"What about him?" said Jane. She was pointing north beyond the quayside, to a lone fisherman who looked ready to set off in a small vessel.

"Run!" Kate yelled.

They did so, off the stone and brick quayside and across the mud.

"Mr Harper!" she called. "Hello! Mr Harper!"

Roger Harper looked up.

"Mrs Forbes?"

A few minutes later, with all explained, he was happily rowing them into harbour waters.

"Lovely day," he said.

"Yes, it is," said Jane.

"That's a good one," he said, indicating an impressive yacht at anchor a little way off their port side. "Not been here long, that one."

There were often two or three yachts in Sandham, usually there for repair or maintenance work. They were rarely as classy as this one though.

Kate squinted to read the name on the bow – 'Helios'. She could also see that the man in the cap on the rear deck was Peter Langham.

"That's Mr Langham's yacht," Kate explained to Roger. "He's in Sandham with his sister."

"It's an impressive sight," said Roger, admiringly. "Must be a 120-footer."

Being as near as they would get on their way across the water, Kate thought it worth taking the opportunity.

"Mr Langham? It's Kate Forbes and Lady Jane. Roger here is taking us across to the other side."

"A pleasure to see you again!" Peter called back.

"We're still looking for our friend. We may as well check the Holton side."

"Good luck then. It's a beautiful day for being out and about."

Kate whispered to Jane. "Perhaps we should be bold. He can always deny it."

Jane nodded and called to Peter. "We were at the church earlier. The vicar says you were asking after Norman."

"Ah… yes, it occurred to me it's everyone's duty to help. It didn't lead to anything though."

"Ah well," called Kate. "Thanks for trying."

"I'm sorry I'm not much help… but it's always good to make new friends. I was thinking… the weather's wonderful… I'd like to invite you aboard this evening. How does a cocktail party with canapes sound? Shall we say seven o'clock?"

Kate was both surprised and intrigued. She glanced at Jane, who was nodding her consent.

She called to Peter again.

"We'd love to. How shall we…?"

"We'll have high tide, so come to the quayside."

"Righto," called Kate.

They were moving away now. Too far for continued shouting.

"Cocktails, eh?" said Roger, rowing effortlessly across the water. "That'll be nice."

"Yes," said Kate.

She wasn't about to get too excited though. A man was dead and now this suspicious chap was luring them onto a boat at night.

Twenty

Just after seven o'clock on a beautiful Wednesday evening, Kate and Jane arrived at the quayside where Helios was moored. It was a stunning prospect: a magnificent yacht, barely a breeze, and still almost three hours of daylight remaining. Jane once more looked resplendent, this time in an emerald-green satin cocktail dress, while Kate had donned a stylish lightweight burgundy cardigan over a cream dress. Both wore sensible flat sandals.

Having enjoyed sausage and mash at five, Kate felt ready to tackle a cocktail or two. That said, she wasn't too keen on a late night. The walk around the Holton side of the harbour and back home had taken forever and produced nothing but aching feet.

Thankfully, any apprehension they may have felt about spending time on a boat with Peter Langham was eased by the presence of several familiar faces on board – namely, his sister, Beatrice Fry, Max Drexler, Teresa Alvaro, Sir

Gerald Clifton, and Stefano Passoni. Indeed, it was a most friendly atmosphere as they were helped aboard by a beaming Peter in a white dinner jacket and Beatrice in a glorious ruby red evening dress.

"I'm so glad you could come," said Peter. "I've rounded up a few friendly faces you might recall. Strangers yesterday, friends today."

"Yes, lovely," said Kate.

"Welcome aboard," said Beatrice.

"Thank you. It's so much easier when the tide's in."

"Yes, the captain's going to take us out a little way for privacy. We'll return in an hour or two while the depth is still favourable."

"She's a lovely boat," said Jane.

"She certainly is," said Peter. "It's in the blood. My grandfather owned a yacht."

"Is this one by any chance a 120-footer?" Kate asked.

"Ah, a boat afficionado. Yes, 121-feet with a steel hull and teak superstructure, a reliable engine, five cabins, as well as space for our crew of four, and a full-displacement hull that means she's very stable when anchored."

"Marvellous," said Kate, looking around. Helios was genuinely spacious and stately – the essence of luxury.

"Not that we're sleeping aboard," said Beatrice. "We prefer hotel suites when possible."

"Yes, and why not. The Crown is a lovely hotel."

Following a more general hello to those aboard, Kate and Jane were soon armed with gin slings and chatting more freely with their hosts while the yacht moved a couple of hundred feet off the quayside. Many subjects were covered and they learned a little more. Beatrice was a widow. Her husband died during the War. Confirmed bachelor Peter, however, had been too old to fight, for which he was grateful. Their grandfather was Austrian; Langham was an English name Peter took during the hostilities – despite being born English, it had proved difficult to bear a name from a hostile country.

But the whole time, Kate was looking for a way to get the conversation onto the subject of Norman West. It was just a matter of being patient.

A while later, the crab canapes were served.

"Mmm…" said Kate, "what's the recipe?"

"Our chef uses bread slices toasted and cut into smaller portions," said Beatrice. "Then on top, the crab, lemon, spring onion, cucumber, mayonnaise and parsley."

"It tastes so fresh."

"The crab was caught earlier under the lighthouse rocks," said Peter. "I sent a man out in the rowing boat with a line."

"An ancient ritual," said Jane. "Fishing and agriculture is the story of all our coastal towns before the Industrial Revolution."

"Ah, then factories gave us a new generation of wealthy men."

"Yes, times are changing," said Jane. "Many lords and ladies remain as fine as they ever were. But others… not so lucky."

"The weather is so much better now," said Kate. "Will you sail off again? Somewhere exotic and exciting, perhaps?"

"We're in no hurry to leave," said Peter. "There's an auction on Friday, remember."

"Ah yes, the auction. Our friend Norman knows a thing or two about quality items. We were hoping he might guide us, but alas…"

"He's still missing then?" said Beatrice.

"Yes, although I don't think Jane and I are the only ones interested in finding him." Kate fixed her gaze on Peter. "Thanks again for taking an interest."

Once again, if Peter had been caught out, he didn't show it.

"As I said earlier, I learned nothing."

"Yes… Jane and I were surprised that a visitor should go out of their way to ask the vicar about Norman's whereabouts. I was thinking of mentioning it to my friend, Inspector Ridley of Scotland Yard – purely to coordinate all the avenues of inquiry that have so far been taken."

Suddenly, Peter seemed a little less certain of himself.

"Yes, well, perhaps I should have mentioned a minor association with Mr West. I paid in advance for his valuation services, but he hasn't reported back. Obviously, his wellbeing is the main thing, but I'd be keen to speak with him."

Just then, Sir Gerald Clifton joined them. He somehow looked at home standing on a yacht in a dinner jacket.

"Marvellous boat. A real beauty. I've never considered it before, but standing here… I wouldn't mind having one myself."

Jane engaged with him.

"We were talking about Friday's auction."

"Yes, I'm very much looking forward to it."

"Is your associate an expert in fine things?"

"Which associate…?"

"The boxer chap."

"Oh, he's not with me. I hardly know him."

"Oh, our mistake. We're so absorbed with finding Mr West, we're liable to get things the wrong way round."

"That's alright, Lady Jane. Think nothing of it."

Twenty-One

Thirty minutes later, those aboard had become three groups, with more drinks and louder voices. Peter and Beatrice were now chatting with Sir Gerald, Stefano was with Teresa, while Kate and Jane were getting their first crack at Max Drexler, who looked dapper in a dark blue two-piece suit.

"I do hope you're enjoying your stay in Sandham," said Kate. "It's usually a good place to visit."

"It's a fascinating town," he responded. "There are quite a few things of interest."

"Surprisingly, one of things people seem to be interested in is Norman West, our missing friend. That's not an interest of yours though…?"

"No."

Jane smiled. "I understand you're from Switzerland."

"Yes, I live in Geneva."

"It's always fascinating to hear about other places. I'm sure we'd love to hear about Geneva."

Max shrugged. "What can I say? It's a city… and also beautiful. It's where the Rhône exits Lake Geneva. And what else? The League of Nations has its headquarters there."

"The League of Nations?" said Kate.

"Yes, they hope to bring about world peace. We can only wish them well."

"How do they go about such a mission?" Jane asked.

"I believe they aim to settle international disagreements through negotiation and arbitration, but its workings are a mystery to me. My own interests are in finance."

"Sandham must seem small to you," said Kate.

Max laughed in a kindly way. He had charm, and Kate could see why Miss Alvaro was intrigued by him.

"No, Sandham does not seem small. Yes, I live in the city, but I come originally from St. Moritz, a small community on the other side of Switzerland. It's on an Alpine slope below the Piz Nair overlooking Lake St. Moritz."

"I've heard of it," said Jane. "The Winter Olympics?"

"Yes, that's right. I have family and friends there who helped host the Games. It was quite an event. Terrible blizzards at first and then it became too warm. But we're ready for anything there, of course. We have fine hotels and electric trams. And our visitors? In the summer, they walk, sail, and play golf. And in the winter, there's ice-skating, curling, bobsleigh, and skiing."

"Ah, skiing," said Kate. "I understand Mr Langham would like to learn."

"Yes, I know some enterprising people in St Moritz who are planning to open a ski school for foreign visitors."

"That's a novel idea," said Kate.

"It's true. They hope to be ready for next winter. I suppose if it's popular, more will open."

"And what about languages?" said Jane. "I hear Switzerland has quite a mix."

"Yes, where I live in Geneva, people speak French. But in St Moritz, half the people speak German, a quarter Italian. Some still speak the old Romansh dialect."

"And you speak all of them?" Kate wondered.

"I do. And a little English, of course."

"Excellent English, I must say. You're a fine ambassador for your country."

"And you for yours."

"Well, it's really only Sandham I can influence."

"Oh, but this is how it begins! When my grandfather was young, St Moritz had only summer visitors. Then, his friend Caspar, a hotel owner, made an offer to four British guests. If they came back in the winter and disliked it, he would pay their costs. And if they enjoyed it, they could stay for free as long as they liked. This one hotel owner created winter tourism in the Alps and, right away, my grandfather opened a tourist office, the first in Switzerland."

Cogs began to turn in Kate's head.

"Now there's a thought for Sandham. A visitor information office…"

"May we join you?" said Stefano Passoni, looking a little warm in a grey woollen suit. He was with Teresa Alvaro, who looked effortlessly classy in a midnight blue silk woven fabric cocktail dress.

"Of course," said Kate, stepping aside to widen the circle.

"We were talking about tourism," said Jane.

Stefano smiled broadly. "Oh, you'd love Italy. I've been over there many times and can recommend the weather, the wine, the food... and Italy gave us the puppet show on the beach."

"Punch and Judy?" questioned Kate. "I thought that was an old British tradition."

Stefano shrugged. "Punch is a Neapolitan character. Pulcinella."

"It is," said Jane. "In England, it dates to the reign of Charles the Second. Also, Samuel Pepys mentions it in his diary. So, over two hundred and fifty years ago."

"You're a student of history," said Stefano, looking pleased. "We could talk for hours, I'm sure."

"Ice cream," Teresa interjected. "We enjoyed ice cream on the prom."

"That's also Italian," said Stefano. "I might be English, but I'm proud of my heritage."

"I too had ice cream," said Max. "A strawberry cornet. Very refreshing, although perhaps not as refreshing as a swim in the sea. It looks warm but I know it's freezing."

"I think the idea is to take a deep breath first," said Kate.

"Yes, my wife is a wonderful swimmer," said Max.

Kate hoped she wasn't staring too hard at him.

"Will you be at the auction?" Jane asked him, thankfully changing the subject.

"Yes, I'm a collector, so there might be one or two interesting items."

"It's the same for me," said Stefano. "I thought this auction might be just the thing for my new London home. Country house furniture is just what I need."

"Is that why you're looking for Norman West?" asked Kate. "Winnie at the tea rooms thinks you're lovely, by the way."

Stefano hesitated before replying.

"Yes, I may have mentioned Norman. The thing is I'm always interested in meeting anyone who's discreet and knows the value of things. To be honest, I need help. Otherwise, I'll spend far more than I need to."

"And Miss Alvaro," said Kate. "Are you looking forward to the auction at all?"

"Yes, I'm interested in old English furniture. Like Stefano, I also have a new home in London, so something beautiful would be perfect."

"I know what you mean," said Jane. "A friend of mine recently moved into a new home and is having trouble choosing pieces."

"Yes, absolutely. Is your friend in Sandham?"

"No, in London. There are so many places to buy furniture and art there, it's difficult to make a choice. Have you shopped around in London?"

"A little, yes, but when I heard there would be country house furniture for sale here, I had to come. One never knows when something interesting might become available. And of course, I'm to be married soon."

Kate's eyeballs attempted to pop out, but some kind of superpower allowed her to limit her reaction to a twitch.

"How lovely. Is your fiancé in Sandham?"

"No, in London. Jeremy works in finance. I'll be back with him this weekend."

Kate swallowed drily.

"Well, it's wonderful to hear. I do hope you're both very happy together."

Twenty-Two

On a glorious Thursday morning, aunt and niece set out from home. While Kate embraced summer with a yellow outfit, the thinnest cream cardigan and a large white handbag, Jane had opted for a sky-blue blouse, billowing cream trousers and a cream shoulder bag. Both were wearing sensible shoes.

"Hopefully, our potential visitor attraction will be intact enough to be a success," said Kate on the short walk from Cobb Lane to St Matthews.

"Don't get your hopes too high," Jane suggested. "Time is usually the enemy in these situations, and that fresco is old."

Approaching the church, they found the vicar waiting for them just inside the entrance.

"Good morning, ladies. Shall we?"

They followed him to the chancel. Here, behind the altar, stood a richly decorated, free standing, Victorian screen – large enough to cover an earlier altarpiece background fixed to the wall in the form of a frame covered with wooden panels. The decoration on this had faded badly.

A middle-aged man stood beside it.

"This is Ben Evans, our handyman," said the vicar.

Once the introductions were completed, Jane had a question for the vicar.

"How long has it been covered?"

"According to church records, the frame was fixed to the wall in 1720. The freestanding screen was put in front of it in 1852."

"We had some repairs done to the 1720 one in 1911," said the verger, approaching suddenly from behind them. "Some of the panels were loose."

"Before my time," said the vicar.

"Not before mine," said the verger. "I was here. It's a dusty old mural behind it, that's all."

"A historical artefact," said Jane.

"Exactly," said Kate. "It might draw in those interested in our history."

"Right then," said Ben. "Shall we…?"

He used a long iron crowbar to gently lever away the loose end board. Then he levered away another.

"Yep, a fresco," said Jane, peeking behind.

"Let's go a little further," said the vicar.

Ben applied the tip of the bar to the next board. This one, being firmly fixed, groaned noisily as he pried it away from the frame.

"That's fabulous," said Jane.

"A rare thing indeed," said Kate, assessing the growing revelation.

"Keep going, Mr Evans," said the vicar, by now a little excited.

Soon, a third of the twenty or so boards had been removed to reveal a vista, somewhat faded, of a saint on a rock looking down on a ship on a rough sea.

"A fresco for Sandham's seafarers," said Kate.

"Most likely painted straight onto wet lime plaster," said Ben. "It's an old technique."

"Italian Renaissance," said Jane.

Ben nodded. "Yes… it's not so much a painting on the wall; it's more a part of the wall. If the conditions are right, these can last for centuries. This one could be four hundred years old."

"Ben's right," said Jane. "I was lucky enough to visit Rome. Even a small, out-of-the-way church might have the most fascinating age-old frescoes."

"Do we think it's a viable visitor attraction?" said Kate.

The vicar considered it.

"It's quite lovely… but faded perhaps a little too much. Don't you think?"

"It's old," said Kate. "Of course it's faded. Clearly sea faring was a subject for prayer in Sandham. It's part of our history, vicar."

The vicar considered it a little more.

"You've convinced me, Mrs Forbes. It's an attraction. Perhaps not one for permanent exhibition, but we'll remove the 1720 frame and move the 1852 screen back a little to keep it covered. Only those who come to peek behind will see it."

"For which we'll charge a penny," said the verger.

"Perhaps we could pray for those at sea," Jane suggested.

The vicar smiled.

"Dear Lord, we pray for those at sea. May they know that you will hear them at all times, in calm and storm. We pray that they be protected and sail without fear, knowing that you are watching over them. Amen."

"Right," said Ben, "I'd better get on with it then. I'll patch up any damage as best I can."

"Perhaps the verger could assist you," Kate suggested. "By holding things."

The verger took a patient breath before accepting the task.

"And what of Norman West?" the vicar asked. "Any progress?"

"Not really," said Kate. "I'm beginning to think we've wavered in our search. Look at us, celebrating history when a soul might be lost to us. He could be at the bottom of a cliff, or unconscious in a ditch, or lost in the wilds…"

"Have you tried the pub?" said Ben, preparing to loosen a panel.

"The pub?"

"He plays dominies with the landlord of the Spotted Dog, Bertie Naylor."

"Oh, thank you, Ben," said Kate. "That's very helpful."

Twenty-Three

In bright sunshine, Kate and Jane reached the end of the High Street furthest from the quayside. This was known locally as the St Mary's end, due to the presence of the Catholic Church. Its neighbour was Bertie Naylor, landlord of the Spotted Dog pub, a popular hostelry which opened for business at eleven o'clock in the morning.

Kate was outside checking her watch.

"Ten to…"

She was about to tap on the window when the door swung open.

"Oh…" said a surprised Bertie. "I thought it was one of my more enthusiastic customers."

Kate smiled. "Hello, Mr Naylor. We're looking for Norman West. I assume you've heard he's missing?"

"I have, but he's not staying here. If I'd seen him, I'd have told the police."

"Absolutely. No one's suggesting you're hiding him. May we come in."

"I'm not open yet."

"We're not here for the beer, Mr Naylor."

He stepped back to let them in.

"I'm not sure I can help, ladies," he said, heading behind the bar.

Kate and Jane followed as far as the customer side.

"Is there anything you can tell us about him?" Kate asked. "Anything that might give a clue to his whereabouts?"

"I don't think so. I mean he's good at dominoes. I'd say he's been playing for years, if that helps."

Jane smiled. "We were thinking more about Norman West, the man. Did he ever mention anything about his life before he came to Sandham? His family, friends, the people he worked with?"

"Not that I recall. He was always keen to talk about the here and now more than the past. Then again, a pub landlord is like a Catholic priest. The confessional is… you know."

"Sacrosanct?" Jane prompted.

"If I start telling you everything I've heard, I'd end up with no customers."

Just then, the door swung open and in walked Inspector Ridley.

"Mr Naylor…?" he managed to say before his eyes adjusted to take in Mr Naylor's visitors. "I trust you ladies aren't investigating my case for me?"

"Good morning, inspector," said Kate. "We're merely looking for a missing friend."

"Yes, well, once again I must warn you to tread carefully. In fact… come outside a minute."

They followed him into the street and down the pub's side alley for privacy.

"This could be a dangerous situation you're getting involved in."

Kate frowned. "What, finding Norman?"

"I can't say too much, but we have certain persons on file. Please take this warning seriously."

"Your files?" said Jane. "Would they relate to Sir Gerald Clifton, or Peter Langham, or Beatrice Fry, Stefano Passoni, Teresa Alvaro, or Max Drexler?"

Ridley didn't look particularly pleased.

"Why give me those names?"

"I'm sure it's nothing, although they were very good company last night."

"Last night?"

"We were on Peter Langham's yacht, Helios."

"It's a 120-footer," Kate added.

"Norman West's name came up several times," said Jane. "It might be worth looking into."

Kate raised a hand. "Just don't say we sent you."

"You should also talk to the boxer chap," said Jane. "Sir Gerald pretty much denies knowing him, but something doesn't quite add up there."

"Yes, well, the boxer is Frederick Tanner. That's all I can tell you. Now, I'm busy looking into a murder and I insist you keep out of it. I won't ask you again. Next time, I'll take action."

*

Somewhat chastised, Kate and Jane arrived at the Promenade Tea Rooms in need of a fortifying cup of tea. Before they could enter though, a familiar figure emerged from the Crown Hotel across the street.

"Sir Gerald, hello," Kate called to him.

"Hello to you too," he replied, seemingly without a care in the world. "Another fine day."

"That was a pleasant evening on the boat," said Kate.

"It was. And now I'm off on another pleasant engagement. A trip to the auction rooms."

They waved him farewell and watched him head up Royal Avenue.

"The boxer," said Jane. "Frederick Tanner. What if Sir Gerald's telling the truth. What if Tanner doesn't work for him."

Kate considered it.

"They definitely have some kind of business relationship, Jane."

"I agree, but what if it's not as we see it? What if Tanner is a freelance operative. What if his little chats with Sir Gerald aren't a man reporting to his boss, but a man negotiating with another?"

"It's an interesting idea, but not one Inspector Ridley would encourage us to look into."

Jane nodded. "Obviously, we're not investigating Mr Benson's murder…"

"No, we're not. We're merely looking for Norman."

"Here's a question then. Is Tanner staying at the Crown Hotel?"

Kate shrugged… and then popped into the hotel, where Sally was looking bored behind the reception desk. Kate asked about Tanner.

"That kind of information is confidential, but no. He was chatting to Sir Gerald a while ago, but he's not with us."

Kate thanked her and returned to Jane with a report.

"Here's an idea then," said Jane.

"Strictly relating to Norman?"

"Yes, strictly relating to Norman."

"Go on."

"What if Norman isn't hiding from Tanner? What if he knows him. What if he's staying with him?"

"Oh Jane, what a thought. The boxer and Norman… friends. Yes, what if this Tanner chap is hiding our Norman?"

"He's not staying at the Crown, so we're looking at a smaller hotel or a boarding house."

"There's plenty of those in Sandham."

"A boxer shouldn't be too difficult to locate. Someone will know."

They entered the tea rooms, where Winnie greeted them from behind the counter. Kate smiled back at her.

"Two restorative teas, please, Winnie."

"If it's energy you need, how about a piece of Madeira cake? Enid's been baking."

"Ah no, thank you – we're having lunch with Lady Davenport and Mrs Howard later. Don't want to overdo it."

"Righto."

"You might be able to help us with some information though. We're looking for a man named Frederick Tanner. We think he might be a former boxer. He certainly has the look of someone who's taken too many blows. That said, I get the feeling he's dished out a few. He's not staying at the Crown, so it'll be one of the smaller hotels or a boarding house."

"Frederick Tanner…" mused Winnie.

"He tends to wear smart suits."

"Well, Maggie's daughter does a bit of cleaning in a few of the boarding houses for those who can't or won't do it themselves."

"Maggie?" said Jane.

"Maggie at the quayside souvenir shop. Dolly's sister."

"Right."

"You sit down and have your tea. I'll send Enid. She got you into this mess. She can make some inquiries."

"Did I hear my name?" came a voice from the staff room.

While Enid went off, Kate and Jane sat down by the window. There, they enjoyed a cup of tea, and also caught sight of Max Drexler leaving the Crown Hotel opposite.

Twenty-Four

Half an hour had passed with nothing much happening – apart from Winnie, Ernie and three others taking the opportunity to question Lady Jane.

"You mean he wasn't good enough?" said Winne from behind the counter. She was referring to a certain viscount Jane had been engaged to.

"You can't marry a man who's not good enough," said Ernie.

Kate had already given up and could only shrug. Jane was fine though. And perhaps she was right to answer these questions, if only to put the matter to rest.

"He's a good man," said Jane. "But we weren't a good match. When he revealed his evil plan, I had to call it off."

"Evil plan?" echoed at least four people.

Kate had never seen such a rapt audience, not even at the Alhambra.

"I'm sure you don't want to know," said Jane.

"We do, we do!"

Jane glanced at Kate. Was that a glimmer of mischief in her eyes? It was gone in an instant.

"Alright but prepare to be shocked."

Ernie Melton took a fortifying slurp of tea. Winnie held a cleaning cloth to her chin, perhaps ready to hide behind it.

"It happened one afternoon," said Jane. "We went to visit a house he wanted to buy. It was to be our marital home. The location was perfect, just southwest of London in beautiful grounds. Are you sure you want to hear all this?"

"We do!"

"Alright then. The neighbourhood was wonderful. The house was ideal. But things went very badly once we stepped into the magnificent library, its shelves bearing a thousand books the previous owner had left behind, and yet with enough space for another thousand books of my choosing. I almost swooned with joy. But then… his words will haunt me forever."

"What words!"

"He said… Don't worry, I'll soon rip this lot out. It'll make a terrific billiards room."

The collective gasp was followed by the door swinging open.

Enid was back.

"Mrs Price, Shore Way," she puffed.

Kate and Jane left promptly.

"Mrs Price's boarding house then…" said Kate as they crossed the street – but their progress was halted by Peter and Beatrice leaving the hotel.

"Off out and about?" Kate inquired.

"We're going back to the boat," said Peter. "I could do with a spot of rowing. One cocktail too many last night, I think."

"Well, thank you again for a lovely evening."

"You're welcome," said Beatrice. "It's nice to make new friends."

Just then, Teresa Alvaro emerged from the hotel.

"A little gathering?" she asked.

Peter explained his and his sister's plans, while Kate said that she and Jane were off to see a friend.

All then broke up.

Mrs Price's boarding house was halfway down Shore Way, one of the streets that ran from Back Lane to the promenade. None had a sea view – that was generally the nature of boarding houses.

Kate and Jane had no trouble finding Mrs Price – she was outside sweeping her steps. Kate did the introductions and then got to the point.

"Do you have Frederick Tanner staying here?"

"What's all this about? I've already had Constable Harris come round asking the same question, but he wouldn't say why."

"We're not part of any police investigation."

"No offence, but I didn't imagine you were."

"We're simply looking for Norman West. He's not staying here, is he?"

"Don't be daft! Of course he's not staying here."

"Is Mr Tanner in?"

"No, he went out a little while ago. Why?"

"Could we check if he's hiding Norman?"

Mrs Price was almost dumbstruck. "Hiding him…?"

"Yes, hiding him."

"Which room?" asked Jane.

"Second floor… front room."

Kate and Jane were quickly there, but the room was empty.

Jane sighed. "If Tanner's not hiding him, then we're better off going back to our earlier assumption – that Norman could be hiding from Tanner."

"Jane? Do you think Tanner killed Mr Benson?"

"It's possible."

"It's a good job we're not investigating it. Otherwise, we'd be saying Sir Gerald Clifton knows something about it."

They returned to the street where Mrs Price was about to come back in.

"Do the police know you're looking for Mr Tanner?" she asked.

"No," said Kate. "Inspector Ridley would have us locked in a cell before you could say Welcome to Sandham."

"I see."

"Do you know which way he went?" Jane asked.

Mrs Price peered down towards where the street met the promenade.

"That way," she said. "He turned right at the end."

They thanked her and departed.

Before they reached the end of the street though, a familiar figure went by on the promenade.

"It's him," said Jane. "He knocked at Swift House the other day."

"Yes, the bearded man – a suspicious individual if ever I saw one. He said he was looking for Norman."

"It could be innocent," said Jane.

"Yes, possibly, although with this whole business, there's less and less that can be described as innocent."

They reached the end of the street and took a nearby bench on the promenade. Ahead of them, on the shingle and sand, people were out in numbers enjoying the sunshine. Kate wished they could join them.

"Thinking of Mr Tanner," said Jane. "Before we completely close down any possibility that he's not friends with Norman… what if Tanner knows where Norman's holed up and has gone to meet him?"

The not-too-distant church bell at St Matthew's began to sound midday. Before it finished, Kate and Jane were marching towards the western end of the promenade, where it split into two paths – one up to the lighthouse, the other to the harbour shore and, a little further along, the quayside.

As they turned towards the harbour shore, Kate puffed.

"I'd love to say I'll be glad when we've found Norman and can get back to normal… but I have a feeling that that finding him won't be the end of it."

She was upset. This rotten business threatened to spoil everything for the town's visitors, who were out in force, taking strolls by the harbour, admiring the boats, enjoying the sunshine. Indeed, coming along were two familiar faces. Kate and Jane smiled at the maroon couple as they passed, this time both wearing grey.

The first stop, once again, was Mr Chivers' old boat house with its cracked window.

"Back again?" he grumbled.

"Sorry," said Kate. "We're still looking for Norman West. Only, we think he might have other people looking for him too. People he might not want to meet."

"Whereas we're friends," said Jane. "He's not staying in your boat house, is he?"

Mr Chivers' face darkened.

"No, he's not! Now clear off before I fetch the police."

They withdrew without delay.

"That went well," said Kate.

"Look, Peter Langham." Jane was indicating a rowing boat approaching Helios, where a crewman was waiting to help him aboard. "Last time we saw him, he and Beatrice were heading back to the yacht."

"But Beatrice is already aboard – there on the deck. He must have taken her to the yacht and rowed away again."

Their next stop was the Royal National Lifeboat Institute boat house. Crewman Joe Cullen had finished varnishing the south-facing side and was now on a stepladder addressing the north side.

Kate explained their continuing mission, but Joe could only shrug. He even invited them to take a look, which they did. But Norman was neither aboard Guinevere nor hiding in the equipment cupboard.

Next, they came to Bill Thornton's repair yard. He and his apprentice, Albert, had begun to rub down the rowing boat that had previously been covered with a tarpaulin. Only, they were absent.

"Probably gone to lunch," said Jane.

Once again, it seemed unlikely that Norman would be hiding in Bill's establishment, but they looked anyway – without any luck.

They pressed on towards the next building – the large one capable of sheltering two or three small craft. Before they got there though, they found a body.

A snoring one.

They passed by Ned Dawson, who had found a spot in the long grass behind the shoreline path. His battered old chair was outside the boat house, but there was no sign of life anywhere. They entered through the shoreside door.

The window on the south side lit up two small boats on trailers and cast dark shadows between them.

Kate called out.

"Norman?"

There was no answer.

She stepped forward and stopped.

"There's someone here," she whispered.

She stepped forward again and gasped as a furry interloper scooted past and out through the door.

"That's twice we've almost given each other a heart attack."

"That's not fair," said Jane. "He's got more lives than you."

"Oh… there's something else."

"Not another cat?"

"No, a man. I think he's dead."

Jane hurried to her aunt's side. And there between the wall and a boat, lay the body of Frederick Tanner.

Just then, someone appeared at the door.

"Stefano?" said Jane.

He gave a cheery hello and came in. But then his mood changed.

"Ladies? What have you done?"

Twenty-Five

A short while later, Stefano returned with Sergeant Jones and Dr Howard.

While the doctor examined the body, Jones took the opportunity to express his disappointment.

"Why am I not surprised to find you both here?"

Kate shrugged. "Believe me, sergeant. We'd prefer to be anywhere but here."

"According to Mr Passoni, he found you with the victim."

"Yes, I don't suppose there's any point in telling you we were looking for Norman West?"

"A blow to the head," said Dr Howard.

"Most likely that oar," said Jones, indicating one lying on the ground a few feet away.

"Poor Mr Tanner," said Jane.

"Yes, poor Mr Tanner," said Jones. "Our chief suspect in the Benson murder."

"He was ours too. Not that we were investigating."

"Where's Inspector Ridley?" Kate asked.

"In Brighton," said Jones. "Advising on another case. He'll be back soon. In the meantime, did you see anyone suspicious on your way here?"

"Yes, Mr Passoni."

"I'm not suspicious," said Stefano. "I was merely nearby."

"We did see a bearded chap on the promenade earlier," said Jane. "He knocked on Norman's door a couple of days ago. He wears a straw hat, glasses, light suits, bright ties. He speaks well."

Jones frowned. "I'll look into it."

"Ladies," said Dr Howard, "you must be upset. If you need a sleeping draught later, you know where to find me."

"A stiff brandy will suffice," said Kate.

Jones huffed. "We'll have that reporter back. We won't look good, that's for sure."

"No, I suppose not," said Kate.

"Can't stand reporters. There's always a queue to talk to them, just to get their names in the papers. When I walk in, it goes quiet. We'd solve more crimes if we said we were reporters."

"The freedom of the press is vital," said Kate. "Even if it's occasionally a nuisance."

"Yes, well, I'll take your statements, ladies, then you can go home and keep out of it."

*

Kate set off south along the harbour path past the many small boats beached on the shore. Jane was just behind her.

"Aunt? The quayside's the other way."

"I know…"

Yes, the quayside led to the High Street, which led to Cobb Lane and Kate's home, but she needed time and space to think.

"It's such a lovely day, Jane."

"It is," said her niece, moving alongside her.

"So much for getting people to visit Sandham. Who'd want to come here?"

"It'll take time, but anything you can do to improve the town's appeal will resonate far into the future. Max Drexler's grandfather opened a tourist office, the first in Switzerland."

"Now's not the time, Jane."

"I know… but progress needs visionaries. Your time will come."

"Visionaries. Honestly, Jane, that's the last thing I am. I'm just an interfering… well, I poke my nose in where it's not needed. And I think I do it to give myself some kind of rhyme or reason."

"You know what we need? Lunch."

"Possibly, but this whole business… we've been going at it all wrong. It's time for a fresh approach."

"Yes, a fresh approach and a sandwich."

Kate smiled. "Yes, we're due at Pru's soon. I might have to cancel it though. She's an absolute diamond, but polite chit-chat is the last thing we need."

Just then, from the long grass beyond the path, came a groan. This was followed by Ned Dawson stirring and sitting up.

"Ladies?" he questioned.

"Ned? I'm sorry to say there's been another murder."

Ned roused himself and came to join them.

"What's happened?"

Kate's explanation had Ned in shock.

"I usually sit outside on guard, sort of thing. Just think, it could be me dead in there."

"I'm sure that was never likely, Ned. Still, you'd best let Sergeant Jones know you were present. He'll want to ask if you saw anything suspicious."

"There wasn't anything suspicious. Had there been, I'd have leapt into action. Old navy man, y'see. Always alert to danger."

While he headed back to the boat house, Kate turned to face the water.

"Look, Jane – there's Peter and Beatrice."

She and Jane waved – and as they did so, Ned came back.

"There *was* one strange thing. A bloke with a beard, glasses, straw hat and bright yellow tie came asking about Norman."

"When was that?" Jane asked.

Ned checked his watch.

"Half hour ago."

They thanked him and resumed their stroll.

"Let's get this right," said Kate. "Mr Benson was killed at the cottage. We thought Tanner might have been the killer, but now someone's killed him. What really happened?"

"Let's take it a step at a time, Aunt. Firstly, Norman's not a double killer. He'd have risked being seen."

"Yes, it's even possible he's a victim we've yet to find."

They reached the fork in the path. Up to the right was the rise to the lighthouse where a dozen or so holidaymakers were milling around. They turned left and took a bench on the promenade, just in front of the public gardens.

Here they sat in quiet contemplation. Perhaps there was too much floating around in their heads, because both, at one point began to set out a scenario only to halt and fall back into silence.

"How about that sandwich?" Jane eventually said.

But suddenly, Kate's mind was on something else.

"Look who's coming along."

Jane turned to see Max Drexler and Teresa Alvaro coming from the direction of the harbour.

"Hello," Kate called to them.

"Hello," said Max as they approached. "Miss Alvaro and I were out walking alone and bumped into each other by the lighthouse."

Kate waited until they were close.

"There's been a murder."

"No!" gasped Teresa.

Understandably, the reaction was one of shock, followed by questions, which Kate and Jane answered as best they could.

Although the lighthouse was some two hundred yards from the murder scene, Kate thought it worth asking anyway.

"Did you see anything suspicious?"

Max raised an eyebrow.

"I really think you should leave it to the police."

"Yes, Sergeant Jones said pretty much the same."

"Good day, ladies."

Kate watched them stroll on, waiting for them to be out of earshot.

"Jane, someone around here is a killer. Someone we've met, I'm sure."

She looked up to the lighthouse. Had Max and Teresa really been up there?

"Aunt? We were about to have a sandwich."

"Yes, of course."

They left the bench and headed east along the promenade, taking it slowly to avoid catching Teresa and Max who were a little way ahead.

"What do we make of Teresa Alvaro?" Jane wondered.

"I wish I knew," said Kate. "On the one hand, she and Max could be having an affair. On the other… I'm not sure what."

"A violent attack by Teresa seems unlikely. We're looking for someone with greater physical strength."

"She could be paying Max as a hired assassin. It doesn't get us very far though. If we *were* investigating a double murder…"

"Aunt, we *are* investigating a double murder. Whether we like it or not."

"Yes, well… in that case, I think we're stuck."

"Possibly, but Sir Gerald's man, Tanner is dead, and yet Sir Gerald told us he barely knew him. I find that very suspicious."

"Me too."

While Max and Teresa continued past Royal Avenue towards the cliffs, Kate and Jane stopped on the corner outside the Crown Hotel.

"Speak of the devil…" said Kate.

It was Sir Gerald Clifton approaching the hotel from Royal Avenue.

"Hello, there," said Kate. "See anything new at Wilson's?"

"What? Oh, yes, one or two things. I'd say they're pretty much set for tomorrow. Now, I don't know about you, but I think some lunch is in order."

They watched him disappear into the hotel.

"He's right about lunch," said Jane.

Before they could make a move though, someone called out.

"Ladies," greeted Ernie Melton coming down Royal Avenue. "Bargain hunting always gives me an appetite."

"Don't tell me," said Kate. "You've been to Wilson's and identified an unknown Rembrandt."

"Not quite, but I've got my eye on a lovely vase. I can't say which one, of course."

Kate had a sinking feeling.

"Vases are a very poor investment," she advised.

"Was it busy at Wilson's?" Jane asked.

"Oh, planning to sneak up there, are you?"

"No, but you might be able to help. How long were you in there?"

"Not too sure. An hour or so? Maybe longer. It's no crime to do a bit of research."

"While you were there… did you see Sir Gerald Clifton? He's the one we saw with the boxer."

"What, in Wilson's?"

"Yes, while you were in Wilson's."

"Oh, I get it… you want to know what he's looking to bid on. Well… come to think of it, no, he wasn't there. And that business… you know, when I said he looked like a crook. I hope we can forget that. I didn't know he was a Sir then."

Kate turned to Jane.

"We'll have that sandwich, Jane, but first I'll telephone Pru with our apologies."

With that, she popped into the Crown Hotel to make the call.

Twenty-Six

Thankfully, no one in the Promenade Tea Rooms was reading aloud from the newspapers. Editors were quick to move on to fresh stories, meaning Sandham was out of the national spotlight. A brief respite, Kate feared.

"We were just discussing men," said Winnie, indicating her sister Enid, Colonel Pickering and Ernie Melton. "What's a lady to look for in a suitor?"

Kate had no wish to discuss men and presumed Jane didn't either. But Winnie continued all the same.

"Love?"

"A man of means," said the colonel.

"Yes, money," said Ernie.

"Certainly, a man with prospects," said Winnie.

"Yes, and money," said Ernie.

"And he should be from a good family," said Winnie.

"Yes, one with plenty of money," said Ernie.

"I don't suppose you had any luck with Mr West?" said Winnie.

"No… no luck." Kate thought it best to avoid mentioning the second murder.

"We'll keep looking," said Jane.

"I know some of his friends," said the colonel. "Not personally, but I know who they are, sort of thing. Old work friends and such."

"Do you know where he worked?" Jane asked.

But Kate beat him to it.

"The Harvey Nicols store in London. He mentioned it once when he first came to Sandham. I've always remembered it because I once bought a hat there. It made me realise that I'd been in the same building as Norman West ten years before I met him in Sandham. It struck me in a philosophical way, although I'm not sure why."

Whatever the reason, a noisy Norton CS1 motorcycle pulling up outside halted any further reflection. It was Colin Nelson from the Sussex Chronicle.

"News travels fast," said Jane.

He was quickly inside.

"Mrs Forbes and Lady Jane?"

"Never heard of them," said Kate.

"One of the locals let me in on it. I don't think the police were in a hurry."

"It only happened an hour ago."

"What did?" asked Winnie. She seemed to be speaking for the other six or seven people in the tea rooms at the time.

"I've just come from the police station," said Colin. "I heard you two were at the scene."

"Must dash," said Kate. "Things to do."

They were quickly outside and heading up Royal Avenue.

"There's some bread at home, Jane. We'll make toast."

They half expected Colin Nelson to follow but, instead, it was Stefano Passoni they saw, up ahead, coming towards them.

"Ah, Stefano."

"Hello there!"

"I hope you don't think we're being rude," said Kate, "but what were you doing at that boat house?"

He seemed to weigh it up.

"I can't say too much but I'm suspicious of certain people."

"Who?"

"Stay out of danger, ladies, and let me know if you find Norman West."

With that, he continued towards the Crown.

"Inspector Ridley should be back from Brighton soon, Jane. There are one or two things we haven't told him because they seemed unimportant. I think the situation has changed."

*

It was just before one o'clock and Inspector Ridley, just back from Brighton, was eating a chunky cheese and pickle sandwich. Kate noted how he ate slowly and deliberately, much the same as he walked. Always a man to leave space for thought and reflection. A good detective.

"That looks a fair sandwich," she said.

"Constable Harris's mum obliged me. Cheddar cheese and a chutney she makes with apples and cider. Marvellous. Why aren't you at home?"

Kate's stomach rumbled.

"After we left Sergeant Jones, we saw Max Drexler and Teresa Alvaro coming back from the lighthouse."

"Shall I jot that down, sir?" Harris asked.

Ridley nodded, but Kate wasn't finished.

"We also saw Peter Langham in a rowing boat near the crime scene, Sir Gerald Clifton returning to the hotel from the auction rooms, except we have a witness that says he was never there. And as for Stefano… well, you'll have heard about him being close by."

"And don't forget the bearded man," said Jane. "We told the sergeant about him."

"Yes, well, thank you."

"If there's anything more we can do to assist…?" Kate offered.

"No, and I'll ask you again to keep away. This is a dangerous business."

"And a complex one. You're looking for someone who will kill as they need to but has an outwardly pleasant persona."

"Is this intuition, Mrs Forbes?"

"My late husband used to say there's no room for intuition in deciding a person's fate, but that it's not a bad place to start when seeking the evidence to do so."

"I've heard that before… actually, it was you who told me."

"Can't you share anything with us?"

Ridley put his sandwich down.

"All I can tell you is it's looking very much related to some long-standing unresolved matters in our files. I can't say more, so please don't ask me."

Kate and Jane departed, although, thanks to the open window, just managed to hear the inspector asking Constable Harris, "How come they know more than we do?"

"It's probably fair to say Norman knows a thing or two about valuable items," said Jane as they walked away.

"It certainly explains why people might want to talk to him, but it doesn't explain why two of them are dead."

"Unless we're dealing with something that's valuable enough to kill for."

Before long, they were back at Kate's front gate. Only, a relaxing lunch was once again about to evade them.

"I don't believe it." Kate's heart raced. She felt ill.

They approached with caution, keeping a steady eye on the shattered glass panel in her front door, which itself was ajar.

"What if they're still here?" whispered Jane.

Kate carefully pushed the door open and stepped inside. Glass crunched beneath her feet as she selected the heaviest of three umbrellas in the stand.

"Hello?" she called with all the confidence she could muster.

Twenty-Seven

Kate's heart thumped as she and Jane moved further into the hallway. Who might they find? If anyone? It took her back to girlhood when she was tasked with looking for the school ghost in the library, only to have a copy of *Jane Eyre* fall off a bookcase shelf in front of her. Yes, it was obvious later that Hannah Shearer was behind the bookcase with a long stick to poke through a hole in the back, but for three whole minutes young Kate believed in ghosts. It might have been a lifelong certainty had the bookcase not begun to giggle.

Reaching the parlour door, they both peeked inside.

It wasn't a pretty sight. While the room was mercifully empty, things had been scattered about the floor. Frustration and a little anger flared in Kate's chest. This was no time to loiter though.

In this way, they moved slowly through the house – hearts beating, umbrella at the ready. It took several minutes to confirm that the thief had flown.

Back in the parlour, Kate picked up a small drawer that had been emptied out.

"Who could have done this, Jane?"

"Someone who's looking for Norman."

Kate waved the drawer. "They can't have expected to find him in this."

"It's something they believe he has. They must suspect he's given it to you for safekeeping. Just to be clear – he hasn't, has he?"

Kate was alarmed.

"No, of course not."

"It wouldn't have to be recently. It could be something he gave you months ago."

Kate thought hard.

"No, he's never given me anything."

She picked up two of the seven figures that made up a Russian doll set and placed one inside the other.

"At least they didn't break Babushka."

"You know what this means, Aunt? Not everyone believes we're looking for Norman. Someone thinks we've found him, or possibly knew his whereabouts all along. Whichever, they suspect we're in league with him."

"Alright, Jane. Let's be bold. Let's assume this is about a valuable item. Would it be something that's going to be auctioned on Friday?"

"I doubt it's something that can be sold openly."

Kate looked around again and sighed.

"Once again, I'm sorry for getting you involved in all this."

"You didn't. It was Enid Turpin. And we wanted to help, which was the right thing to do. There's nothing to apologise for."

Kate smiled. "Just think, I might have investigated the whole thing on my own."

"I'm glad I was here to help."

"Me too. Very glad indeed." Kate placed the two Russian doll characters on the sideboard, one inside the other. "Now, before we tidy up, I suppose we ought to contact the police. They might want to take fingerprints."

*

While Constable Harris was busy in the parlour, Inspector Ridley was in the dining room with Kate and Jane, who were finishing off belated toasted cheese sandwiches.

"I don't expect we'll find fresh fingerprints," he said. "Both murder weapons were wiped clean where you might grip them, and we haven't found anything to go on at any of the break-ins."

Kate put her sandwich crust down and wiped her hands on a napkin.

"Inspector, someone's trying to get their hands on a valuable item – one they believe Norman West has, or one he's given to someone to look after for him."

"Yes, that second one, Mrs Forbes. Has he passed you anything to look after for him?"

"No, of course not. We've told you everything we know."

Ridley went to the window and peered outside.

"I reckon Norman West has fled the scene. I don't know how, but I reckon he's in London with… well, never mind that. Whoever's responsible for the murders and break-ins doesn't realise he's gone. They will soon enough though. Then we'll lose them too. I'll be honest with you. It's not looking good."

Jane's brow furrowed.

"You said Norman's *with*… would that be a person or an object."

"Sorry, Lady Jane, I can't say."

Now it was Kate's turn to frown.

"Do you have men looking for him in London?"

Ridley turned to face them.

"A small army, yes."

"Well, good luck to your troops in finding him soon. I'd very much like to get back to normal."

"We might not catch him. That's my concern."

Kate sighed. "I suppose it's rare for the culprit to drop directly into your lap. Although Henry once convicted a thief in Arundel who fell into a sergeant's lap."

"From a window?" Ridley presumed.

"No, he stole a bicycle from a shed."

"Oh?"

"The sergeant was walking by and… well, the bicycle's owner had locked it away prior to having the brakes fixed. When the owner shouted, 'Stop thief!', the sergeant raised a hand directly ahead of the would-be escapee."

Ridley no doubt pictured this for a moment before moving on.

"Finding Norman West is important, but my top priority is finding the killer."

"So, you don't think Norman's our killer then."

"No."

"Which means you might have a suspect or two in mind?"

"Possibly, but I can't comment."

Jane put her hands together.

"I know it's none of our business, inspector, but is it also possible you have no real suspects at all?"

"I refer you to my previous answer, Lady Jane."

Twenty minutes later, Kate and Jane waved the police off. Order could now be restored. Except, Kate was reluctant.

"Where shall we start? The parlour or the back room?"

Jane considered it before answering.

"The harbour. Let's start there."

Twenty-Eight

They left the house and headed up Cobb Lane towards the High Street. Kate was in a pensive mood.

"Let's think like the police, Jane."

"Go on then."

"What do we know regarding Tanner's murder? And how does it tie in with Benson's death?"

"It might be worth breaking this down as far as we can go, Aunt. Let's take Stefano, shall we? He was at the boat house."

"Yes, although he turned up after we went in, not before."

"But what if he killed Tanner and left, only to see us coming along? He might have blended with the visitors on the harbour path before coming back."

"Yes, it's suspicious having him show up like that. Let's say it wasn't a coincidence. Let's say he had the opportunity to kill Tanner. And the oar was a readily available means. That just leaves motive, which would be greed regarding an item worth killing for. Can we link him to Sea View Cottage though?"

Jane considered it. "Sea View Cottage… in terms of motive and means, yes. But did he have the opportunity?"

"If we can prove that, Jane, I'd say he's our double killer."

They turned right onto the High Street, bound for the quayside.

"What about Sir Gerald then?" Jane mused. "Means, motive and opportunity. A poker and an oar, and a motive of greed. But what about opportunity?"

"Well, if we're *not* looking for a double killer, then he could have got Tanner to kill Benson… and we know Tanner was familiar with the cottage. He followed us there. The question is, did he know about it on Monday?"

"It's possible."

"Then what if Sir Gerald became suspicious of Tanner? What if he thought Tanner might be double-crossing him? Might he have killed him?"

"Again, it's possible, Aunt. If we're to identify two separate killers, then Tanner and Sir Gerald fit the bill. Of course, at the time of Tanner's murder, Sir Gerald says he was at Wilson's."

"But Ernie Melton says he wasn't."

"Wilson's isn't far from the quayside or that boat house. What if Sir Gerald was bound for the auction preview but changed his mind?"

Reaching Church Lane, they crossed the High Street. From here, its straight line began to twist and turn into the oldest part of town.

"Speaking of two killers then, Jane. What of Max and Teresa."

"Teresa says she wasn't in Sandham at the time of Benson's murder."

"No, but Max was. If those two are working together, then she could be paying Max as a hired assassin. Or… they might be secret lovers looking to set themselves up for a rosy future."

Jane nodded. "They were in the vicinity of the boat house. And Max followed us near the church. We know he was looking for Norman. It's possible he was at Sea View Cottage. Proving it though… that's the thing."

"There's a third double act, Jane – Peter and Beatrice."

"Yes, Peter was looking for Norman. He asked the vicar. He no doubt asked elsewhere. So, in terms of means, motive and opportunity… with Tanner's murder, he was rowing nearby, and the oar was available. But as for motive… that's the weak point. He's extremely wealthy. Why risk his neck?"

"There's also the question of Sea View Cottage. He might have gone there, but there's no evidence."

"Yes, there's a gap regarding Peter Langham."

"What about the bearded man, Jane? He was near the boat house. *And* he called at Swift House. He knew Norman's home address. What if he knew about the cottage?"

"Yes, he's very suspicious. No doubt about it."

"There's also Norman. While I doubt he's a killer, if we look dispassionately, we're bound to say he was at Sea View Cottage and he knows what this entire business is about. He had means, motive and opportunity regarding Sea View Cottage. As for the boat house though…"

"Means and motive, yes, Aunt, but he'd have to come out of hiding. Everyone's looking for him, so to stroll through the town to commit a murder… very risky."

"Hmmm."

Aunt and niece reached the quayside, where a number of visitors were milling about.

"Hello," came a call.

Up ahead, a familiar couple were heading towards them – Fliss and Harry.

"The maroon people," said Kate. Indeed, both were back in maroon, although this time a shirt and a blouse. "Hello!"

"We heard the shocking news," said Fliss. "Another murder! It's really quite worrying."

"Yes, just as well we're moving on," said Harry.

"You're leaving?" said Kate.

"Yes, this afternoon. Hampshire and then Dorset."

"Well… that sounds lovely." Kate couldn't see any reason to hold them up. "Best of luck. And do have fun."

"We will," they said in unison.

She watched them go.

"Jane, have we just let two killers go?"

"No, if we suspect them, we may as well suspect the whole town."

It was nearing the end of lunchtime, meaning that Mrs Dobson's Superior Dining Rooms and the Prince of Wales pub were still busy with visitors and workers. As it was, a face emerging from the pub looked familiar. He was clutching a couple of loaves wrapped in paper.

"Crab canapes," whispered Kate. "He served us on Peter's boat."

"Well spotted, Aunt."

"Good lunch?" Kate asked him.

He stopped, momentarily surprised, but then made the connection.

"No, no, I was just getting bread."

"Ah, thirsty work. Nothing wrong with stopping off for a glass of beer."

Kate was trying to think of the best way to make the most of the opportunity. How could this crewman help them with Peter's movements?

"I'd imagine you've gone ashore for bread in countless towns?"

"Very many, yes."

"It must be fascinating to work for a wealthy yacht owner."

"Yes, Monsieur Marcel is a good employer."

Kate was confused.

"Monsieur Marcel?"

"Yes, a good owner."

"I thought Mr Langham was the owner."

"No, Mr Langham has hired Helios."

"I see… well… we won't hold you up."

But before he departed, Jane stepped in.

"We're thinking of chartering a boat such as Helios. Does Monsieur Marcel have other boats?"

"Yes, but most are smaller."

"And he's based in Paris?"

"Yes, but the larger boats are on the coast at Honfleur."

"Is that what you do? Sail to England and back?"

"No, Mr Langham is taking us to Greece."

"Greece? Well, thank you."

He smiled and withdrew. A moment later, they watched him push the Helios rowing boat into the water and climb in.

"What do we think of that then, Jane?"

"I'm thinking Peter Langham may not be as wealthy as he'd like us to believe."

They left the quayside by heading south along the harbour path. This meant passing the boat house where

Tanner had perished, which made Kate feel uneasy. It also meant passing Ned, who was asleep in the chair outside it.

A little further on, they were level with Helios, which was moored a hundred feet away. The crewman was already halfway there.

"My eyes aren't as good as yours, Jane. Is that Peter Langham on the deck?"

"Yes, it is."

Kate held her hands to her mouth and called out.

"Peter? Mr Langham?"

He turned and waved. "Hello!"

"Have you spoken to the police yet?"

"No, why?"

"There's been a murder!"

"Yes, I heard, but it's nothing to do with me."

"You were seen rowing in the vicinity."

"I've been rowing all around this wonderful harbour. I hope that's not a crime. Now, if you'll excuse me – things to do."

Beatrice came to stand alongside him. But she didn't wave.

Twenty-Nine

Kate and Jane reached the promenade with a thought to try the Crown Hotel, as there would no doubt be a good few still at lunch. Before they got far though, they spotted Colin Nelson, the Sussex Chronicle reporter coming their way.

"Hey, that's a bit of luck," he called. "I've been looking for people who might have some useful knowledge – and here you are."

Kate wasn't in the mood, but he was soon with them all the same.

"We've already explained our position, Mr Nelson. We don't wish to be interviewed."

"Fair enough, but either way you're in my report. I've had plenty of people talk to me, so no problem there. You should hear what they say though."

Kate bristled. "Exaggerated nonsense, I expect."

"Too right, Mrs F. Thing is, you're in a position to help me write something more considered. It's your choice, of course."

Kate sighed. "This is for the Sussex Chronicle?"

"No, I've got a contact in Fleet Street. This is going national. Exaggerated or not."

"Both Jane and I favour accurate and respectful reporting."

"As do I, ladies. I'd love to get the real you in the story. Why don't you tell me about yourselves. A bit of background adds depth."

Kate grimaced but then conceded.

"I'm Mrs Katherine Forbes, widow of the late judge Henry Forbes CBE and sister of the late Annette Scott, Countess of Oxley. My companion is Lady Jane Scott, daughter of my late sister and Robert Scott, the Earl of Oxley."

Colin Nelson jotted notes quickly and skilfully in shorthand.

"And Lady Jane? Someone at the tea rooms said you go around digging up dead bodies."

Jane viewed him calmly before speaking.

"I'm primarily a historian but, at Oxford, Professor Peregrine Nash got a few of us interested in archaeology. He's now based in Sussex, so when there's a chance, I join various local digs. We were recently at a site near Crawley, and come September, we'll be at Penford Priory. Apparently, it's haunted."

"It sounds fascinating," said Colin, noting it all down.

"Historical research is my main interest, so hopefully there'll soon be more of that."

"And is digging an interest of yours, Mrs Forbes?"

"No, as I've told Jane before, I have neither the patience, the eyesight, nor the knees for it. My main interest is Sandham – promoting it to visitors, day-trippers, holidaymakers and so on."

"But I'll get Aunt Kate to Penford," said Jane. "She'll love it."

Kate felt a warm glow.

"Well, if you insist."

"Now, ladies, tell me about Norman West. You've spent the past few days looking for him…?"

The next ten minutes was a flurry of further questions and answers. Then they left Colin Nelson to it.

"He's not a bad lad," said Kate as they made their way to the hotel.

*

Sally was behind the desk when they entered. She looked up with a smile, but before she could speak, Kate fired off a question.

"Is there anyone in the dining hall?"

"A few. Twenty, perhaps."

"We'll take a peek. Thanks, Sally."

They left her looking baffled as they pushed through the double doors.

The hotel dining room was a large space with ornate plasterwork in the classical style, which had been installed only the previous spring. There were around thirty tables mainly set to seat two or four diners. The tableware was also ornate. The hotel owners were champions of the old style, uninterested in the new, plainer, angular designs one was starting to see in magazines.

As predicted by Sally, there were around twenty people seated in various groups, most of them with post-lunch drinks.

The waiter came over and smiled apologetically.

"I'm sorry, Mrs Forbes, but lunch has finished."

"It's alright, we're just looking for a friend. Ah..." She gave Jane a nudge. "I spy with my little eye..."

Sir Gerald Clifton was seated alone at a table for two in a corner, partially hidden from view thanks to a standing trellis and large potted plant.

They made their way over to him, where Kate gave him her best smile.

"Sir Gerald? I expect you've had a busy day?"

"Ladies, I'm about to take a nap in my room, then I'll pop over to Wilson's. It's the final preview. Big sale day tomorrow."

"Yes, a ten o'clock start."

"Still searching for your friend?"

"Yes, we're still looking for Norman, but… we're more concerned that Frederick Tanner was killed."

"Yes, I heard. Shocking business."

Jane frowned.

"Sir Gerald, you went to the auction rooms earlier."

"That's right."

"And yet a friend of ours says you weren't there."

"Lady Jane… Mrs Forbes… you're not spying on me, are you?"

"That's not the point," said Kate.

Sir Gerald smiled generously.

"Well, actually, I had a little change of plan. The weather was so lovely I took a stroll around the church. That's not a crime, is it?"

*

Kate and Jane were soon back on the street and heading up Royal Avenue.

"Well, Jane, we wondered if Sir Gerald was lying about being at Wilson's. Now we know for certain he was. Is it getting us anywhere though? We can't say for sure who killed Tanner and we still haven't found Norman West."

"How about trying Swift House again, Aunt? We never got the chance to go through Norman's things."

"Yes, and here comes the man who threw us out."

Sergeant Jones was coming down the street. On seeing them, he came to a halt and waited for them to reach him.

"Keeping out of trouble, I hope?"

"Yes, sergeant," said Kate. But further up the street, on the other side, she spotted a suspicious figure. "You know, if this whole thing wasn't a police matter, we'd have questioned that man over there."

"What man?" said Jones, turning the way indicated by Kate.

"Him." It was the man with the beard, straw hat and glasses. "He's the one we told you about. He was near the boat house prior to Mr Tanner's murder and, the other day, he knocked at Norman West's house while we were there."

"Right…"

Jones set off at the gallop, calling after the bearded man. There then followed some kind of disagreement between them, which resulted in Jones applying an arm lock before frog-marching the poor chap in the direction of the police station.

"Do the police have their killer?" Kate wondered.

"Time will tell, Aunt. In the meantime, I'd suggest we stick to our plan of going to Swift House. We might yet learn something about Norman."

Thirty

Kate and Jane were on the patio at the rear of Swift House. While the garden looked as stunning as ever, their attention was elsewhere. Denied a front door key by Enid Turpin, who was under police instructions to deny anyone access, they were sizing up an alternative method of entry – the back door that relied upon a heavy bolt to secure it from within.

"It's cardboard," said Jane. She was examining the repair job, where someone had cut and wedged a stiff sheet of the stuff over the broken glass pane.

"It's not proper breaking and entering then," Kate postulated. "Someone else has already done the breaking. We're merely entering."

Jane carefully pushed the cardboard inward, where it fell to the floor. Some of the jagged glass remained in the frame, but there was room for her to snake her arm through and slide the bolt across.

"Nice and tidy," Jane observed once they were inside. "Tilly did a good job."

"She did," said Kate, thinking about her own house. "It was the same burglar, I'm sure. Rest assured, I won't swear and wish eternal damnation on them. At least, not out loud."

They began their search, looking carefully through anything that might tell them more about Norman West.

"The address book's gone," Kate noted.

"Inspector Ridley's probably got that. He won't get any quick answers from it though. It's in code."

"I thought it might be."

"I'd imagine it's a Plus One or Plus Two or Minus Five kind of thing. A is B or E or what-have-you. We girls did that sort of thing at school when we passed notes to each other."

"Did you indeed?"

"It's best if you alternate. Plus Two then Minus One. That would make Kate Forbes… M. E."

"Very clever. I'd imagine it's difficult to crack."

"It is if he uses different codes for initials, buildings, street names, telephone numbers…"

"I did wonder why someone lived at Unqcpg Court in Hewxzij Street."

"Finding Norman won't be easy, Aunt. I mean what do we know about him?"

"He moved to Sandham two years ago."

"And before that?"

"He worked at Harvey Nicols in London."

"What if someone there knows more about him than we do?"

"It's possible."

Jane was soon on the telephone to the Harvey Nicols store, giving a brief outline of her wish to locate Norman West.

Kate meanwhile opened a cabinet door. There wasn't much to see. It was as if Norman lived in a museum. It was lovely, but not homely.

"They're putting me through to the office," Jane reported. She followed this by repeating her request. "Yes, two years ago. Yes… I just wondered if he'd been up there recently to see old friends." Jane's eyes widened. "Oh. Right. I see. Thanks very much for your help."

She ended the call.

"Norman West died six months ago."

Kate was surprised.

"That doesn't make sense – unless our Norman West wasn't a department store worker."

"I think we should keep searching."

It was a good ten minutes before Jane found something intriguing.

"Blank invoices. Hatherley's of Old Bond Street."

She handed a batch to Kate.

"Interesting. How would Norman get hold of these?"

"I'm not sure, Aunt, but I know Hatherley's. It's not far from our place in Berkeley Square. They handle auctions and private sales of paintings, jewels, works of art."

"Hmm, there's no shortage of country houses selling off the family silver."

"Yes, well, Hatherley's offers a discreet service, which is handy if you don't want the world to know you're selling to survive."

"Unlike the unfortunate Brand family at Wilson's."

"They also offer a valuation service, which might be more to the point."

Jane made another telephone call – this one to Mayfair. It took a bit of persuasion, but the name Lady Jane Scott was just about enough to extract an answer to the question 'Do you have a Norman West working for you?'

Kate watched her niece carefully. Jane was one of those people with lots going on beneath the surface that wasn't always apparent unless you looked closely. It was at times like this though, tackling a tricky puzzle, that she came more visibly to life.

"Never? Alright, what about a Reginald Unsworth then?" There was a brief pause. "Oh, that's brilliant. Thank you."

Jane put the receiver back in place.

"They've never heard of Norman West, but Reginald Unsworth retired two years ago. The lady I spoke to thinks he moved to the seaside."

Kate almost laughed.

"Norman West is Reginald Unsworth. The sheer cheek of the man!"

"It seems you didn't know him as well as you thought."

"Jane, I don't know him at all."

"I presume he lied about his past for a reason. Perhaps he didn't want it known he had a background in valuables."

"Where is he right now? That's the main thing."

"We wondered if he might be staying with Frederick Tanner. We were wrong about that, but what if it was the right approach?"

"Right idea, wrong person? Yes, Mr Unsworth rents Sea View Cottage. Only Mr Unsworth is Norman West."

"And Mrs Digby says Mr Unsworth is an ex-army man doing business abroad."

"Except he isn't."

Thirty-One

Mrs Digby looked surprised.

"Mrs Forbes?"

"Mrs Digby! We haven't seen you in ages."

"You saw me yesterday."

"Let me put the kettle on. We want to hear all your news."

They got as far as the parlour door when Alice Digby caught up with them.

"I'll make the tea. You two sit in there. Then you can tell me what all this is about."

"Fair enough," said Kate.

A few minutes later, they were sitting on the settee sipping tea from the best chinaware while facing Alice, who was perched on the edge of one of the two armchairs.

"Now, what's all this about?"

"We have news," said Kate.

"Important news," added Jane. "In fact, so important, we might as well all be in here to discuss it."

Kate put her cup down on the saucer on the low table in front of her. It was time to raise her voice a little.

"You can come out now, Norman."

There was no response, so Kate shrugged a little, picked up her cup again, and took another sip.

"Nice tea, Mrs Digby."

"You're welcome."

Kate put her cup down again.

"Norman? We're still waiting. And I do think you'll want to hear this first hand."

There was a further silence.

And then, out the back somewhere, the sound of movement.

A moment later, Norman West appeared in the doorway.

It made Kate shudder. Was this man a killer? She tried to picture him coming at her with a poker. It wasn't a pretty sight. However, unlike Mrs Digby's description of Reginald Unsworth – mid-forties, tall, a former army officer – Norman was older, shorter, and looked like an accountant.

"How did you know I was here?" His expression was puzzled but cheery. Kate took the puzzlement as genuine, the cheeriness less so.

"That's not important. Quite a few people have been looking for you. The bit of good luck you've had is it's Lady Jane Scott and me sitting here and not someone else."

"Why, what's up?"

It was Jane's turn to put her cup down.

"As you'll have seen in the newspapers, we found Mr Benson at Sea View Cottage."

His demeanour changed. Gone was the false cheer.

"Yes, the whole country knows about it. My advice is stay out of things that don't concern you."

Jane was undeterred.

"You mean leave it to the police?"

"There's no need to tell them anything. I'm innocent. I'm only hiding to save myself."

"You're a murder suspect."

He looked surprised.

"I can't think why. I haven't killed anyone."

Alice cracked.

"I told you to go to the police, didn't I? I said it would bring trouble to my daughter's door."

"Alice, there's a killer out there."

Alice turned to Kate and Jane.

"Norman came to us, desperate. We said we'd keep him safe for a few hours until things settled down. Then it was overnight. Then for a day, then two. We didn't know what to do. He said the police wouldn't hold him as he was innocent, but then this Sir Gerald bloke would get him."

"It's true," protested Norman. "Nothing's changed."

"Well now," said Kate. "If we inform the police, you'll be charged."

"For the first or second murder?" Jane wondered.

"Both."

Norman wilted a little.

"What second murder?"

"A man called Frederick Tanner. We wondered about you having to get across town unseen, but here you are, quite close to the quayside and not far from the boat house where we discovered Tanner's body."

"Ladies, I can't be found. It's too dangerous."

Kate surmised that Norman was either a good actor or he was genuinely afraid.

"Are you sure about Sir Gerald?"

"Yes, he's your killer. Tanner worked for him."

"Is this one lie after another, Norman… or do you prefer Reginald?"

"You know me, Mrs Forbes. I'm no liar."

"Tell the truth then and you'll have nothing to fear."

"Seriously, just get the police to arrest Clifton."

"Why? Currently, there's more evidence against you than there is against Sir Gerald."

Jane nodded. "My aunt's right. You'll be charged by the police, possibly with murder. No jury will have sympathy for someone who hid from the law."

"I'm not hiding from the law, I'm hiding from Clifton."

"The counsel for the prosecution will tell the jury that Sergeant Jones knocked on the door while you were in the house. It couldn't be plainer. Unfortunately, you've made Mrs Digby and Mrs Vincent accessories to your criminal activities."

Norman looked across at Alice Digby, who clearly wished she hadn't got herself involved.

"We should leave," said Jane. "The police can take it from here."

Both she and Kate stood, but Norman blocked the doorway.

"No..."

But now Mrs Digby stood too.

"Let them go, Norman. If they don't go to the police, I will."

"Alright, wait. Just give me a minute to think."

All three ladies resumed their seats.

"Norman?" Kate prompted. "What's it all about?"

He clearly didn't want to tell them – but his options had vanished.

"Alright..." His eyes flicked from Alice to Kate to Jane. "Have you ever heard of the Lombardy Jewel?"

Neither Kate nor Jane had.

"Isn't Lombardy in Italy?" said Kate.

"Yes, but that's not important. The thing is the jewel was stolen in Paris a week ago."

"And now it's in Sandham?" asked Jane.

"Yes, in Sandham."

Kate was baffled.

"What's it doing here?"

Norman sat himself down in the spare armchair.

"I'll tell you."

From his pocket, he produced a stylish silver cigarette case, took one out and lit it with a match. Belatedly, he offered one to the visitors. Both declined.

"I used to work for a London auctioneer and valuer."

"Hatherley's of Old Bond Street," said Jane.

"Yes… well, I liked to shop at Harvey Nicols. That's where I made friends with the real Norman West. Well, not great friends as such, but we had something in common. We were both due to retire at the same time. That gave me an idea. You see, I couldn't afford to retire in any great style, but I knew if I carried on dealing on the side, I could do quite well. There's always a spot of trade available if you know the right people. And I do know the right people."

Kate's eyes narrowed. "And Hatherley's were fine with that, were they?"

"Goodness me, no. I'd meet whoever it was in the pub. No, it was all off the books."

"So, you came to Sandham with a new name."

"There are some funny people about. I'd amassed a decent collection. I didn't want them coming to pay me a visit. Much easier to become someone else, as it were. Obviously, I kept in touch with those I trusted."

"We've seen your address book."

"Yes, well, that won't help you identify them."

"It's a simple enough system of codes," said Jane. "Would people's initials be three back, two forward? That kind of thing?"

Norman paled slightly, while Kate shook her head.

"W. B. became T. D., which was very unfortunate for poor Tessa Draper."

"Let me guess," continued Jane. "Sir Gerald Clifton isn't in your book."

"No, he's not. He's one of the funny people I mentioned. Best avoided."

"Why were you meeting William Benson?"

"Look, if you want to help me, then help the police nail Clifton. Once he's out of the way, I can return to normal."

"What's his role in all this?"

"The Lombardy Jewel. He's the buyer."

"Well, that certainly strengthens the case against Sir Gerald," said Jane. "Do you have it?"

"No, I don't. All I know is Benson brought it across from the Continent, and I was to give it the once-over to make sure it wasn't a fake."

Jane stood up and went to the window. A group of visitors were passing outside, laughing about something as they made for the quayside.

She turned to face the room.

"So, Sir Gerald Clifton agreed to buy the Lombardy Jewel…"

"Yes, he did," said Norman.

"And William Benson had the jewel in his possession, so either he stole it in Paris, or someone else did and he's just a courier."

"He wasn't a thief; he was a regular carrier. I met him seven or eight times previously, bringing items over from certain persons."

"All stolen items?"

"Yes."

"No doubt Sandham works perfectly. It's not as obvious as London, and I dare say you think of the police here as docile."

"It's nothing personal."

"What would Sergeant Jones and his team see anyway? A chap who retired from a department store coming to live in a seaside town that just happens to have a harbour. It's hardly likely to raise their suspicions."

Kate wasn't happy. "Poor Sandham. All this criminal activity going on unseen under everyone's noses."

"Yes Aunt, and it might have remained that way had the Lombardy Jewel not been stolen."

Norman looked agitated.

"That's why the police need to charge Clifton. The jewel's missing and he thinks I've got it. I swear to you, ladies, I haven't – but I won't be safe until he's in jail."

Kate shook her head.

"I think we should take you to the police station."

"What use is that? I'll either hang for murder or I'll go to prison for conspiracy, which is just as bad as I'll be out in a few years and one of Clifton's gangsters will be waiting for me."

Jane folded her arms. "What about the people who were using your services? Peter Langham, Max Drexler and Stefano Passoni."

Norman frowned. "Never heard of them."

"More lies, Norman?"

"I'm no liar."

"Well then," said Kate, rising to her feet, "we'll have to think about what we do next."

Thirty-Two

It was half-past three on a glorious afternoon. Not that Kate and Jane could enjoy it. They were on a bench looking out to sea and wondering about their next move. For Kate, it wasn't straightforward.

"If it was our mission to find Norman, then the mission's over."

"Agreed. Except now we potentially have a new mission. Can we prevent Norman's murder?"

"We probably shouldn't call him Norman."

"Reginald then."

"Actually… I prefer Norman. The trouble he's caused. Two murders. Break-ins. All my things on the floor. Perhaps we *should* leave it to the police."

"It's tempting," said Jane, "but if the police can't find the killer, I wouldn't be surprised if they tip the whole pot of stew into Norman's lap."

Kate wasn't happy. "I have to say Inspector Ridley has surprised me. I thought he'd swoop and start questioning suspects. All those names we've given him. Has he spoken to *any* of them?"

"He's a good detective, Aunt. He'll have his reasons."

"Where does that leave us though? Does Norman deserve saving?"

"Probably not."

"Will we try though?"

"I don't know. And even if we wanted to, I wouldn't know how. He deserves to go to prison. It's just that the real killer might get away."

"That mustn't be allowed, Jane."

"Alright, but let's concentrate on one murder at a time. We have more information about Tanner's death, so... Stefano was at the boat house. Sir Gerald lied about being at Wilson's. Max and Teresa were strolling by the lighthouse. Peter was rowing nearby. Ned saw the bearded man. And let's not forget that Norman's hiding place isn't far from the scene."

"We need to come up with a plan, Jane. It's either that or hand Norman over to Inspector Ridley and wash our hands of it."

"Let's come up with a plan then."

"You know, Henry loved talking to you about cases. He said you have an astute mind."

Jane smiled. "Well, only the mildest of cases. A stolen wheelbarrow or some missing hay. You got the juicy ones."

"You were young."

"I'd be reading in the garden and hear him through the window telling you about a ruthless poisoner while you prepared his cheese sandwich."

"Yes, I can picture that."

"I remember more recently you said you relied on a crossword puzzle for company."

"That was six months after Henry passed away. It's how I felt."

"He used to say you were a magnificent force of Nature."

"He also said my logic was a bit skew-whiffy."

"You know, I sense the old you again. The skew-whiffy logic. The magnificent force of Nature."

"Perhaps… I do feel more confident."

"Confident enough to become part of the town's future?"

"Get myself on the council, you mean?"

"Yes, uncle would approve. I know it."

"It's a lot to think about."

"I wonder what he'd think about what we're up to with this Lombardy Jewel business."

"If we're pursuing justice, we'll always have his support."

Jane frowned. "Are we pursuing justice though?"

"Yes, we are. It's just a shame we don't have a way forward."

Kate looked down the beach. The sound of waves breaking on the shoreline. A few gulls in the air. People playing and relaxing. It was perfect.

She very much wanted to think about other things. Serving the community being one of them. Perhaps she might one day emulate Liz Charlton, who, in 1910, became Sandham's first woman councillor, and went on to become mayor. Liz had retired to Hove since, but it made Kate think – wasn't it time for another woman to balance out the six aldermen and eighteen male councillors currently running the show?

"How are your other notes going?" asked Jane.

"What other notes?"

"The notes you occasionally jot down."

"Um…?"

"Alright then, the notes for the visitors' guide you're writing."

"Jane! I never said I was writing a visitors' guide."

"When Professor Nash is working on a book, he makes notes in exactly the same way."

"Does he?"

"Yes, so how's it going?"

Kate stared resolutely at the breaking waves… and then gave in and took a notebook from her bag.

"I wrote a piece this morning sitting in bed."

"I'd love to hear it."

"Really?"

"Go on…"

"Yes, well, alright then. Ahem… *Situated behind the western end of the promenade, the Fairview Gardens and its many benches…*"

"Sorry to interrupt, Aunt, but Fairview Gardens?"

"The nameless strip of green with the single bench. I'm thinking ahead to what could be."

"Please carry on."

"*…the Fairview Gardens and its many benches offer the visitor a moment to relax and enjoy a sea view in charming surroundings. One bench, the fabled Lovers' Seat, has witnessed blossoming romances over many years…*"

"Sorry to interrupt again, Aunt, but the Lovers' Seat? How did I miss that?"

"It's my new name for the old bench. Think of it. Five or six new benches and the old one we simply rename."

"I see."

"I'm an honest person, Jane, but publicity is a complex game. I thought it might attract young couples to the town."

"Yes, well, I can't quite see many young lovers rushing to use it. It's in plain view of anyone within fifty yards."

"Yes, although, for some concerned parents, that might be an attraction in itself."

"Oh, Aunt Kate, you'd be so good for the council. You're a non-stop whirlwind of ideas."

"Yes, but right now, I'd swap it all for a way out of this mess we're in."

Jane stood up and stretched her arms.

"I fancy a paddle."

Kate was a little surprised, but it seemed as good an idea as any.

"I'll hold your shoes."

They stepped carefully across the shingle and sand to the point where gentle waves were breaking a few feet away. Here, Jane gave her bag to Kate and, balancing on one leg, removed a shoe and a sock.

"Let's think, Aunt. The killer broke into a hotel room, the hotel safe, Swift House, and your house looking for a jewel." She handed the shoe and sock to Kate and balanced on the other leg. "We know that William Benson brought it across from France and it got him killed. If he'd had the jewel on him, the killer would have taken it and fled." She handed the other sock and shoe to Kate and rolled her trouser legs up. "From that, we might say that Mr Benson hid the jewel somewhere."

"It makes sense, but where? Not on the boat that brought him to Sandham. That sailed away again."

Jane stepped into the water.

"Whoa!" It was clearly cold. "Right, so Benson's movements were limited. He went from the harbour to the Crown Hotel to Sea View Cottage. He may have stopped off somewhere else, but we can't say for certain."

"It doesn't help much."

"There's also the business of Norman going missing. The killer must have known about Benson coming to Sandham. Whether they knew he was coming to meet Norman is a different matter. However..." Jane moved into slightly deeper water. "…by openly looking for Norman, we effectively drew attention to him. If I were the killer wondering where Benson had hidden the jewel, I'd be mightily interested to learn that Norman was meant to meet with him. I might wonder if Norman knew the whereabouts of the jewel. No, I'd be sure of it."

Kate nodded. "The question is, who's the killer? Sir Gerald Clifton wasn't desperately upset when Tanner was killed. Are we certain that Tanner was a close associate? If Tanner was a two-a-penny thug, Norman could be right. Perhaps Sir Gerald has plenty of gangsters working for him. Why would he be sentimental? As I said before, what if Tanner was planning to double-cross his boss? And what if Sir Gerald found out?"

"It's possible." Jane took a couple of steps closer to the shore. "Sir Gerald's alibi of being at the auction rooms was a lie."

"Suggesting he'd been to the harbour?"

"We can't know that for sure."

"What about Stefano Passoni then?"

Jane stepped out of the water.

"Having him confront us just after we'd found Tanner's body… yes, very suspicious. Although he presents himself in an unusual way. As if there's some kind of authority behind him."

"Hmm… then we have Peter and Beatrice."

Kate handed over Jane's socks, shoes and bag, and the two ladies began walking back up the beach.

"Yes, Aunt, Peter and Beatrice… They came in by yacht the day before Benson arrived. Perhaps it's a coincidence. That said, Peter was seen rowing in the vicinity of the boat house after Tanner's death. We also know Peter was looking for Norman. At first, I didn't think much of his story about paying for Norman's services, but then we discovered that Norman provides exactly that service. And, of course, Peter isn't as wealthy as we thought."

"Norman said he'd never heard of Peter Langham. That said, I think we're in agreement that Norman's a liar."

"We are."

"Max Drexler then? What do we think of him?"

"It's difficult to separate him from Teresa Alvaro. She says she wasn't in Sandham at the time of Benson's murder, but Drexler could be working for her."

"Or they might be lovers."

"Yes, it's possible. There's definitely more to their relationship than they're letting on. They were at the lighthouse at the time of Tanner's murder. It's not far from the boat house. Who would notice the two of them among the other visitors on the harbour path."

"And, of course, there's Norman. He could yet be the killer. There might even be two killers."

"It's possible, Aunt, but I favour there being a single jewel-hunter who's killed two people along the way."

"Yes, I think I do too."

They reached the bench on the promenade, where Jane took a seat and began brushing the sand off her feet.

"I'm not sure where that leaves us."

"We're not meddlers, Jane. We're seekers of the truth. The Lombardy Jewel went missing in Paris. People are looking for it."

"Sir Gerald visits Paris. He said so in the hotel salon on Tuesday evening."

"Yes, and it's likely he thinks Norman has the jewel."

"Norman says he hasn't."

"He could end up dead, whatever he says."

Jane began putting her socks and shoes back on. "Our problem is trying to solve it all without falling foul of the police."

Kate stared out across the glistening sea.

"Do you know what… I'd love some normality, Jane. The plain moments of the ordinary are so precious when you think about it."

"They are."

"It's the auction tomorrow. That vase… and Caesar… I'm going to bid big money. I'm sure Julius will fit on that shelf. And as for the vase, it'll look a treat on the sideboard."

Jane stood up.

"That's a thought I hadn't considered."

"What is?"

"Your sideboard… you placed the Russian dolls there."

"It's where they live."

"It might be an answer. Then again, it might not be."

"I don't understand, Jane."

"We need to tell Inspector Ridley about Norman, don't we?"

"We do."

"Right, but how about we take a little diversion beforehand?"

Thirty-Three

The coastal path rose quickly from East Avenue up to the cliffs. Seventy miles across the water lay France. It bothered Kate. What number of boats had come and gone between there and here?

She could see one in the far distance, glinting in the sunlight – but no doubt it was engaged in an honest endeavour, like most vessels. It only took a few to spoil things.

Up ahead, to their left, the branch track led them past the back windows and gardens of the Hughes' Gull Cottage and the Frosts' Cliffside. At Sea View Cottage, they slipped down the side path and round to the front door.

It was still wedged shut with a piece of folded card.

Kate pushed. The card fell to the ground and the door swung open.

"Hello? Is anyone home?"

Sea View Cottage remained silent.

A moment later, they were in the parlour.

"The scene of the crime," said Jane.

"Yes."

"A fight."

"Yes, but now we know what it was about."

"Except Benson didn't have the jewel."

"No."

"And it wasn't in the hidey-hole."

"No – not that it's much of a hidey-hole. It wouldn't be impossible to find it."

"True," said Jane, "but I've been thinking about England during Napoleonic times. From what I know of the period, our Government wasn't blessed with unlimited resources. A single revenue man would have been tasked with covering up to five miles of coastline. Their priority would have been to uncover the big smuggling operations."

"So, not small fry?"

"To be frank, small fry smugglers would have been getting rid of their brandy quickly to lords, landowners and landlords of inns. No fingers would be pointed at a cowherd's cottage."

Jane moved the rug. A moment later, they were peering into the empty chamber.

"I still don't understand, Jane."

"The Russian doll gave me an idea. What looks initially to be the complete thing actually hides a smaller version of itself."

"So…?"

"A hiding place within a hiding place?"

"Oh… you don't mean…?"

But Jane was already flat on the floor with her arm in the space, probing, reaching…

"Ah… yes… we have something. Oh…"

"Jane? Are you alright?"

Jane withdrew her arm, got back onto her knees and held up a midnight blue cloth bag. Kate raised an eyebrow.

"Is that what I think it is?"

She held out a hand for her niece to grab. Back on her feet, Jane loosened the cord to open the bag. She then pulled out a gold chain… on the end of which was an exquisitely carved gold pendant studded with a dazzling oversized ruby surrounded by smaller rubies and diamonds.

"Goodness me, Jane. It's stunning!"

"Benson knew of the hidey-hole. That means Norman knows of it. When he said he didn't have the jewel, he was telling the truth. He just forgot to mention he knew where to find it."

"Yes, he's just waiting for the coast to clear. I'll never trust him again, Jane."

They might have left the cottage right away had it not been for Kate's dislike of upheaval and disorder, which required her to pull the rug back into place.

"There… that's better."

"Moth-eaten thing," said Jane, although her gaze lingered on it.

She then bent down and lifted the rug at one end.

"That's odd."

"What is?"

"There's a small hole in the rug."

"You just said it's moth-eaten."

"The hole matches a hole in the floorboard. I didn't see it at first. It's right by a knot in the wood."

Kate stared down at the old floorboards. They were dull, discoloured and damaged with grime and age.

"We need a knife or something sharp."

"I'll try the kitchen," said Kate.

She returned with an item of cutlery.

"It's all I could find."

"A fork's fine."

Jane placed an outer spoke in the gap between two boards to bend it outward. This she wiggled in the hole by the knot until…

"Hey presto!"

She was holding up a small piece of crumpled silver metal.

"What is it?"

"I might be wrong, but I'm thinking there's an outside chance it could prove useful in trapping the killer."

"Jane, the killer used a poker to bash Mr Benson over the head."

"Absolutely."

Thirty-Four

Kate and Jane arrived at the police station, where Inspector Ridley could be heard in the middle of a discussion with Sergeant Jones. Constable Harris showed them into the front parlour office.

"A couple of visitors, sir."

"Ah, you two," said Ridley. "Pointing that bearded man out has proved embarrassing for us all. Especially for Sergeant Jones."

Jones eyed the ladies. He looked fed up.

"The honourable gentleman in question did not take kindly to me detaining him. He made clear two things. One, that trying to sell heirlooms without the world knowing is not a crime, and two, that he's friends with the chief constable."

"Ouch," said Jane.

"He's from a good family that just happens to be in desperate financial straits."

"We'd prefer not to name him," said Ridley. "In fact, he insisted on it."

Kate understood. "No doubt he was looking for Norman West to facilitate something off the records. Alas, another person who won't be giving Sandham-on-Sea a glowing reference. Unless it's all a ruse?"

Sergeant Jones twitched.

"I beg your pardon?"

Kate smiled in the hope of calming him down. It didn't work.

"Sergeant, I'm merely saying that this honourable chap might yet be linked to what's been going on."

"I don't want to hear it. He's a free man. Not a happy one, but a free one all the same. Whatever he gets up to next… I couldn't care less."

Kate held her ground.

"I'm merely stating that selling off his family heirlooms could be a subterfuge. He might even be the killer."

Ridley waved it away.

"We have no evidence to support that. Or any other theory."

Jane tucked a loose strand of hair behind her ear.

"If you'll permit us a moment, my aunt and I might be able to put you in a better position."

"I don't understand."

"Jane means we know what it's all about. The whole thing. The murders, the break-ins…"

"I'm sure you don't," said Jones.

"The Lombardy Jewel," said Jane.

There was a brief but pointed silence on the police side.

Ridley eventually broke it.

"Whatever you've heard, I'm unable to confirm it."

"It was stolen in Paris," said Jane.

"That may be so…"

"And William Benson brought it to Sandham."

"Yes, well you seem to know a lot about it."

"The inspector's keen to find it," Sergeant Jones added. "His bosses at Scotland Yard are kicking up a right old fuss."

"Yes, thank you, sergeant. Needless to say, I'm under a bit of pressure to get my hands on it – wherever it is."

Jane smiled.

"It's a lot nearer than you think, inspector."

"And what makes you say that?"

She handed him the dusty blue bag, which he opened and peered into.

"Good grief!"

He showed it to Jones, who employed a word Kate preferred not to hear from police officers, or anyone else.

"Well," said Ridley. "This puts matters in a different light. Where was it?"

"At Sea View Cottage," said Jane. "Along with this."

She handed him the small metallic item.

"A bullet," said Ridley. "I thought we searched the cottage."

"We did, sir," said Jones.

"It was difficult to find," said Jane. "I got lucky."

"You're very generous, Lady Jane," said Ridley.

"It might help you nail the killer."

Jones gave a little chuckle.

"Lady Jane, I have to say you're barking up the wrong tree. Nobody was shot with a gun at Sea View Cottage."

"Correct," said Ridley, "but I suspect Lady Jane is suggesting there might have been a struggle."

Jane nodded.

"Norman deals in valuable items. The bullet could suggest a disagreement that ended with a shot, a dropped gun, an iron poker and a dead man."

Jones gave a little shrug. "Makes sense."

Kate gave a polite cough.

"Inspector, weren't you going to tell us everything you know about this whole sorry business?"

"Was I?" He studied the jewel and the bullet. Then he sighed. "Alright, the Lombardy Jewel belongs to Viscountess Lamberg, the widow of Hans von Lamberg, who was an Austrian viscount. It's worth ten thousand pounds."

Both Kate and Jane gasped.

"A fortune," the sergeant confirmed somewhat unnecessarily.

"Yes, indeed," said Ridley. "The Viscountess discovered its absence while unpacking her bags at a Paris hotel."

Kate spotted a connection.

"Sir Gerald Clifton is a regular visitor to Paris."

"So we believe," said Ridley. "Anyway, she arrived there on the Orient Express from Vienna so it's possible it went missing on the train."

"Well," said Kate, "at least you'll be able to get a message to Paris to tell the poor viscountess her jewel is safe."

Jane turned to her aunt.

"What makes you think she's in Paris?"

Kate's brain tried to catch up.

"You mean…?" She faced Ridley. "Is she in Sandham?"

"I couldn't possibly say."

Kate's eyebrows shot up.

"She *is* in Sandham! Well, I'll be…"

Ridley handed the bag to Harris.

"Lock this away, constable, and do not leave the building. Sleep next to it if you have to."

"Yes, sir."

Ridley didn't look happy though.

"We might have the jewel, but there are still two murders to be solved. There's a problem though. Whatever conspiracy's afoot, I'm concerned our suspects will all be gone once the auction's over. The one they're all pretending to be interested in."

Jane puffed out her cheeks.

"We've given you a good few names, inspector. Have you interviewed any of them?"

"Sergeant Jones has been quite busy."

"I meant have you spoken to any of them yourself?"

Ridley paused before answering. "Not personally, no."

"Is it part of a plan you're following?"

"I can't comment."

"Right… if you're to solve this case, every single suspect must be persuaded to stay in Sandham."

"With respect, Lady Jane, I'm not in a position to charge anyone. I mean I can't hold all of them. You're not suggesting that, are you?"

"No, a lack of evidence would soon see them all free again. I'm suggesting we create a situation where the killer stays in Sandham of their own free will and feels assured enough to reveal their identity to us. Possibly tonight."

"Oh really? You have something in mind, do you?"

"I might, but first you'll need to come and meet Norman West."

Thirty-Five

Alice Digby's expression was one of shock. She had just opened the front door to Kate, Jane, Inspector Ridley and Sergeant Jones.

"We just need a word with Norman," said Kate.

Before Alice could reply, they were letting themselves in.

"Back already?" said Norman as he poked his head out of the front room doorway. But his face dropped. Immediately, he turned away and took on the characteristics of an Olympic sprinter. As he disappeared out through the back, a door slammed. Ridley and Jones were already in pursuit.

Jane and Kate followed, although the latter conceded defeat on reaching the back door only to see Norman already disappearing over the back wall. Ridley and Jones went over too.

Kate soon joined Jane, standing on a bench against the wall and peering over. In the narrow alley that ran behind the house, Sergeant Jones was sitting on the flattened would-be escapee.

"Now, what's all this about, Norman?" a breathless Ridley demanded. "Or do you prefer Reginald?"

A few minutes later, all were back in the parlour with a cup of tea.

"Let's get a few things straight," said Ridley. "You've been renting Sea View Cottage for a couple of months."

"Yes," said Norman.

"So how often do you handle stolen goods from the Continent?"

"I don't know what you mean."

"Let me try again. How often… do you handle stolen goods… from the Continent?"

"I don't handle them. I simply authenticate items and give a valuation."

Jane raised an eyebrow. "There's nothing authentic about those blank sales invoices you stole from Hatherley's."

Norman looked uncertain.

"Stolen goods from the Continent?" Ridley repeated. "How often do you… authenticate them?"

"A couple of times a month."

"You went to a lot of trouble renting a cottage."

"It was convenient."

"For crime?"

"Look, I was only going to rent it for a couple of years until I could afford to properly retire. In the meantime, I didn't want certain types of people calling at my house."

Ridley checked to see that Sergeant Jones was jotting it all down.

"Mr West… Unsworth… whatever… you're part of an international conspiracy. Everyone involved is going to prison for a very long time. However…"

Norman suddenly looked hopeful.

"However?"

"Your sentence could be reduced if you help the police."

"That's what I've been trying to do all along. I said so to Mrs Digby and her daughter. I told them I'm desperate to help the police bring the whole sorry business to an end."

Kate had to suppress her distaste. Clearly, Ridley was doing the same.

"I want to know everything."

"Yes, inspector, of course."

"Let's start with the Lombardy Jewel. It was reported stolen by a lady in a Paris hotel. The thief is currently unknown, but it was brought to Sandham by William Benson."

"Was it?"

"Norman, you're severely trying my patience. That won't end well."

"Look, I don't know anyone in Paris. Nor do I want to. Nasty people, according to Benson."

"You told Mrs Forbes and Lady Jane that Sir Gerald Clifton was the buyer."

"Yes."

"How do I know you weren't the buyer?"

"What?" Norman looked genuinely shocked. "I couldn't afford it. It's worth a king's ransom."

"Benson had the jewel though?"

"Yes."

"But someone got to him before you did?"

"Yes. He was a friend."

"Don't give me that rubbish. He was no friend. He was a criminal associate."

"Yes, well, a criminal associate then."

"You've explained yourself to these ladies, now explain yourself to me. What's your true role? I mean apart from conspiracy to obstruct the police during two murder investigations."

"I haven't obstructed anyone. I was in the spare bedroom the whole time."

"Not good enough, Reginald."

"I'm a valuer, that's all. I deal with wealthy people on a 'no questions asked' basis. It tops up my pension. Clifton's your man. A Paris contact of his let him know the jewel was available and he agreed a price."

"Alright, let's suppose it's true."

"It is, although you must understand I usually handle much smaller stuff. I mean the jewel is a big deal. Too big. I've never been involved with anything like it before."

"And now it's led to two murders."

Norman bowed his head.

"Yes, well, whoever killed Benson stole it. They'll be long gone by now. You'll never see it again."

"You're forgetting the break-in at the hotel," said Jane. "Whoever killed Benson didn't get the jewel. That's why they turned his room over and broke into the hotel safe. They also broke into your house and Aunt Kate's house."

Norman shook his head.

"I'm appalled. I truly am. There are some real low-life villains out there."

"Yes," said Jane, "but none of them have the Lombardy Jewel."

"You don't know that. Clifton and his man Tanner knew it was coming in from the Continent and now Benson and Tanner are dead. Someone's obviously stolen the jewel, leaving Clifton to think it's me."

"No one has the jewel, Norman," repeated Jane.

"You can see why I was right to hide. You do understand that, don't you? I won't be safe until Clifton's in jail. What I don't need is to be arrested for my perfectly innocent, very minor role in a slightly shady business."

Ridley eyed Jane.

"Put him out of his misery."

Jane nodded.

"Norman, I found your hidey-hole."

His eyes flicked around wildly.

"What hidey-hole?"

"The one at Sea View Cottage."

"I don't know anything about it."

"It was empty."

For a moment, Norman's eyes flickered with a glimmer of hope – but Jane had more to say.

"Luckily, I had a second look. That's when I found the hidey-hole within the hidey-hole."

Norman slumped where he sat.

"Drat."

"So whoever killed Benson didn't get the jewel."

"Don't worry," said Ridley, "it's perfectly safe in police custody."

Norman came back to life.

"That's wonderful news! I'm so pleased to hear it."

"No, you're not," said Ridley. "There's a good view front and back at the cottage. Benson would've been looking out for you. When he saw someone else coming, he knew where to hide the jewel. He'd been across from France a few times. You must have showed him the hide-away, just in case."

"No, that's not true."

"Let's be honest. You were hoping Sir Gerald would go to prison then you'd go and collect the jewel once it had all died down."

"The thought never crossed my mind."

"Really?" said Jane. "You said you're fearful of Sir Gerald because he believes you have the jewel."

"Yes."

"But it never occurred to you to tell the police where it was hidden. That would have got him off your back."

"Well, to be fair, at the start the police had no idea I was involved. It's only you and your aunt's interfering that put me in their sights. Endless reports there were of you two looking for me. It was like a curse. I can't tell you how much I despised you both."

"Yes, well, Aunt Kate and I don't bear grudges."

Ridley sighed.

"Alright, I've had enough of this. Norman, Reginald, you're a liar and a crook. Let's call Mrs Digby in, shall we. See if she recalls having a hidey-hole in her parlour floor at Sea View Cottage."

"No, please don't trouble Alice. She's innocent. Look, when I first rented the place, she told me about it as if it were funny, but I could see its usefulness. Only… this was different. When I saw the body, I panicked and ran off."

"Benson fell on the rug over the trap door," said Jane. "Was that a factor?"

"I wasn't going to move a dead man."

"Because you didn't want to leave forensic evidence?"

"No, I was worried the killer might still be about."

"But he wasn't."

"No, he must have followed Benson, but he obviously didn't know about our meeting. I assume he searched the place then left. Then I came along and… well… you know the rest."

Ridley took over.

"Where did you go?"

"I went the long way round, into the country and hid in a barn. When it was dark, I came down the riverside path to the harbour, and I asked Mrs Vincent and Mrs Digby for a place of safety. I've done them favours in the past."

Jane rubbed her hands together. "Inspector, if you arrest Norman, Sir Gerald will vanish. You'll have nothing."

Kate concurred. "Likewise, all the other suspects will disappear too."

Ridley sighed.

"I'd love to throw every charge I can at you, Norman. But that won't get me a double killer."

Jane piped up.

"Then don't reveal the jewel's been found."

Norman gasped. "Whoa, hang on, that keeps me in danger."

But Jane's eyes were on Ridley.

"I have an idea, but I'm going to need your help, inspector."

"Hold on a minute, Lady Jane. I'm not handing the investigation over to an amateur. A talented amateur admittedly, but an amateur all the same."

"I think I can talk the suspects into staying on," said Jane. "You'll just have to trust me. And hopefully, they will too."

"I don't know about that..."

"Inspector, one of us needs to persuade them to stay. You're welcome to try."

"Yes, well... what did you have in mind?"

"I'm working on it. As I said, I'm going to need you to trust me."

Ridley glanced at Sergeant Jones who was vigorously shaking his head in the negative. The inspector turned back to Jane.

"You know my thoughts on allowing amateurs to take the lead."

Kate wasn't having it.

"Inspector Ridley, you have within your reach a double murderer. Jane is obviously best placed to give the whole thing a final shove. As there really isn't another way, take what's on offer with good grace. That's my advice."

Ridley scratched his head. He was clearly under pressure.

"Yes, possibly then... but if I agree, there's something you need to factor into your calculations. There's an undercover police operative involved."

"I thought as much," said Jane. "Is that why you've been holding off?"

Ridley nodded. "I couldn't afford to be a cat among the pigeons. A lot of work was done before I got involved. I have to say it's been frustrating for me to stand back, so it's good to hear of any way we can get a result."

"Right then," said Jane. "Let me start by saying I think I know who the killer is."

Ridley's eyes widened.

"Who?"

"Don't worry about that for now. I just need to make an international telephone call… and there's a key we'll need… and if Norman wouldn't mind being used as live bait… oh, and if you could let me have the Lombardy Jewel…?"

Thirty-Six

Entering Wilson's Auction Rooms, Kate and Jane were met with twenty or so bargain hunters taking a final look at the Brand family's possessions.

Despite the general air of enthusiasm, Kate felt sad. These treasures had recently been part of someone's home. Yes, the Brands had to pay off death taxes and debts, but this was a collection a hundred years in the making. Seeing people pore over it seemed…

No, it was fine. These items for sale would find new homes. As for the Brands, their new life was already under way. Sometimes, a philosophical view was the most appropriate. Nothing could last forever.

"Still not sure?" asked a familiar voice.

Kate turned.

"Mr Melton, you surprise us yet again. I'm really no expert so I'll go for something that takes my fancy. In the end, it doesn't matter whether it's a bargain or not, it's knowing it will look nice in my house."

Jane smiled at Ernie.

"I'd imagine you've already worked out what to bid for."

His face lit up.

"Oh yes, Lady Jane, as you rightly say, I know what I'm doing. A couple of shrewd bargains, certainly. But as for showing them off at home – no, I'll sell them on for a tidy profit. It's called business."

"Yes, well, best of luck with it," said Kate, dismissively.

Ernie scoffed.

"Keep an eye on me tomorrow morning, Mrs Forbes. You might learn something."

Kate watched him blend into the crowd and wondered if he'd ever served any useful purpose in life.

"Jane, save me from murderous thoughts relating to that man. What's our first move?"

"How about we reflect our suspects' method back at them."

"I don't quite follow."

"Each of them is hiding behind a plausible story. Let's admit we've been doing the same."

"Oh… right."

"How about we start with Sir Gerald."

"You do the talking, Jane. I'll stand alongside in support."

They approached Sir Gerald Clifton at a display table, where he seemed fascinated by a glass fruit bowl.

"Ladies," he said with a smile. "There's so much to choose from, isn't there. I can't make my mind up at all. Who knows, I might not bid for anything after all."

"You never know," said Jane. "There might be something that comes up unexpectedly. The kind of thing that takes one's breath away. The kind of object that, when we see it, we wish we were the only person in town with the chance to buy it."

Sir Gerald's fixed grin dissipated a little.

"I'm not quite with you."

"A man as astute as yourself won't have been fooled. You know Aunt Kate and I have been looking for a missing person. But you'll also have worked out that our search hasn't been purely down to concerns for a friend."

Sir Gerald wouldn't be drawn, but his eyes showed interest.

"Go on."

"We've found him."

"Your friend? Oh, that's marvellous. Is he well?"

"He's in the pink, Sir Gerald. And you wouldn't believe the surprise he had for us. That item I mentioned, the one you might wish to purchase above anything else? It's available."

"At the right price," Kate added.

"I'm sorry, I don't understand what you're suggesting."

Jane shrugged. "We'll leave you in peace then… and also with this thought. We're in possession of a valuable object from Paris and we'll be splitting the proceeds from its sale with Norman West or, if you prefer, Reginald Unsworth. He's one and the same. After the sale, Norman will disappear, the buyer will disappear, and my aunt and I will forget everything that's happened. If, on reflection, you find our story interesting, why not pop back here after closing time. Let's say seven o'clock. We have a key to the back door, so come in that way."

"Ladies, as I say, I really don't understand any of it."

"We'll be here at seven. There's no need to bring your money. Just a commitment to buy what we show you."

With that, they turned away and made for neutral ground by the larger items at the back.

"He doesn't seem very interested," said Kate.

"It's alright, Aunt, he just needs time for his natural greed to take over."

From their vantage point, they watched Sir Gerald pretend to take an interest in an armchair.

"He has a lot on his mind," said Jane. "Who's next on our list?"

"Mr Passoni? He's loitering over the far side."

"So he is."

"What if Sir Gerald sees us speaking with him?"

"Perfect. He'll be jealous. Let's go and say hello to Stefano, and let's make sure Sir Gerald knows we're serious."

They were quickly alongside Stefano, who was casting an eye over a backgammon set.

"Found anything interesting?" Jane asked.

"Ah, ladies. Yes, I've found something interesting. Sandham itself. I find your little town intriguing. It's not Milan or Paris, but it's beautiful when the sun shines. I'll do as you ask, Mrs Forbes. I'll tell everyone to come here."

"Thank you," said Kate. She wondered – was this really a criminal? It was hard to tell.

"You have the beach, the harbour, the picture house… does Sandham have a football team?"

Kate was surprised.

"Yes, it was originally Sandham United, but the various factions within it couldn't get on. We now have Sandham Town and Sandham Rovers. We get a hundred spectators at some games. Do you follow a team?"

Stefano laughed in a friendly way.

"Yes, some enterprising Englishmen established a Milan team, so I've taken an interest. I was at a recent match with Internazionale, our rivals. Thirty-five thousand in the stadium. Quite a noise. Although Milan lost."

Kate was impressed.

"Well, the Italians gave us Punch and Judy, and ice cream. I'm glad we were able to give something back in return."

Stefano turned to Jane. There was a glint in his eye.

"Do you follow football, Lady Jane?"

As far as Kate could tell, there was the faintest hint of a blush in Jane's cheeks. Undoubtedly, this was a handsome and intriguing man, with a life that embraced much of Europe.

"Perhaps the history of it," said Jane. "Imagine centuries ago… games of football in open countryside… hundreds of players facing each other, one whole village against another. Who would get the ball and bring it home? It could get quite rough."

"You paint an active picture. Perhaps we could have dinner tonight? I'd love to hear more of your thoughts on history."

Kate suddenly recalled the time she had three-freshly-baked cakes and only two cake stands, and the time she, Pru and Ginny were caught in the rain but the taxi could only take two, and the time…

"I'm busy this evening," said Jane. "Aunt Kate and I have a valuable object in our possession which we intend to sell."

"It recently came over from Paris," said Kate. "We'll be splitting the proceeds with our friend, Norman West. After the sale, he'll disappear, the buyer will disappear, and my niece and I will forget all about it."

"I see," said Stefano.

"Come back at seven," said Jane. "We have a key to the back door, so come in that way. There's no need to bring money. Just a commitment to buy what we show you."

With that, they left him to it.

"Right, who's next?" said Kate.

Jane looked around. "We'll have to try elsewhere. Don't forget to smile at Sir Gerald as we leave. I'm sure he heard most of what we said to Stefano."

Thirty-Seven

Slanting sunlight blazed through the upper half of the main windows. The lower halves were covered with shutters, although Kate was able to peer out through a gap. Perhaps she would see someone coming along. Someone who would slip down the side alley and emerge around the back.

Naturally, she was concerned. She and Jane had been waiting anxiously in Wilson's since a quarter to seven. It was now five minutes before the hour. Their first visitor was due imminently. Suddenly, the plan seemed far more dangerous than it had when her niece explained it.

The back door handle rattled, causing Kate's heart to thump.

The new arrival looked a little uncertain.

"We're over here," said Jane from the other side of the main room beside the auctioneer's desk.

The bearded man nodded and came over, taking a seat at the back of five rows which had been set out for the following morning's auction. He pushed his spectacles up his nose a little but kept his straw hat on.

A couple of minutes later, the back door opened again. In a dinner jacket and bright green bow-tie, Sir Gerald wasn't exactly dressed for an illegal encounter.

"I'm still not sure what this is about. I'm in town hoping to pick up a bargain. If that's what you're offering, I come as an honest potential buyer."

"Absolutely," said Jane. "Perhaps you'd care to take a seat."

Sir Gerald squinted against the glare as he headed for a seat in the back row at the opposite end to the bearded man.

"Now what?" he asked.

"The item in question will be revealed soon. Don't worry, it'll be well worth your while."

The back door opened again.

This time there were three arrivals. Max Drexler, Peter Langham and Beatrice Fry. Again, all three had dressed for dinner rather than nefarious activity.

"We bumped into Max outside," said Peter. "I still don't quite understand though. My sister and I are highly respected citizens. I trust this is all above board?"

"Please take a seat," said Kate. "All will soon be revealed."

They did so.

"Where's Norman West?" Max asked.

"All in good time," Kate insisted.

No sooner she had said it, Teresa Alvaro entered. She looked classy in evening wear.

"Ah, Miss Alvaro."

"I see I'm in good company. I hope I haven't held up proceedings."

Sir Gerald fumed. "You haven't. We're stuck in here like a clutch of hens."

"Brood," Kate corrected him. "It's a brood of hens, or if male *and* female, a flock. A clutch of eggs is fine. You can have that."

"I'm not interested in eggs!" Sir Gerald blasted.

"No, indeed," said Kate. "But a little patience goes a long way. Let's not forget that."

"Are we all here?" asked Peter.

"Possibly," said Jane. "We did invite one other interested party…"

Jane halted as the door opened. Stefano Passoni had dressed casually.

"Ah, Mr Passoni! Before you join us, perhaps you could slide the bolt across. We don't want any uninvited late arrivals."

"As you wish."

Stefano bolted the door and then headed to a couple of large wardrobes against the back wall.

"I hate surprises," he said.

Having checked them, he came over to join the others.

"So, why are we here?" Beatrice asked.

Sir Gerald huffed. "Something to do with furniture, I believe."

"If that's the case, let's get on with it," said Stefano.

Kate had heard enough declarations of innocence.

"We all know why we're here."

With the situation growing a little tense, she could feel her heart thumping. Jane meanwhile stood behind the auctioneer's desk, squinting a little into the low sunlight.

"I expect some of you are using aliases, but I'd like to say welcome to you all – the proposed buyer of the Lombardy Jewel, Sir Gerald Clifton, Norman's back-up buyer should things have fallen through, Thomas Smith, then we have interested parties Max Drexler, Teresa Alvaro, Peter Langham, Beatrice Fry and Stefano Passoni. Thank you for accepting our invitation. Each of you is tied to the Lombardy Jewel, recently reported stolen by a lady in a Paris hotel. And each of you is here to take possession of it."

A silence fell – but not a lengthy one.

"Never heard of it," said Sir Gerald. "Whatever Norman West has said is a lie. However, if it's valuable…"

A bang!

All attention was instantly on Jane, who had brought the auctioneer's gavel down on the desk's oak top.

"Five centuries ago, the Visconti family created the Duchy of Milan. It became prosperous and expanded its reach. By the 15th century, it included the region we know as Lombardy. This was then ruled by Habsburg Spain, and following an inter-family war, by Habsburg Austria… until Napoleon took possession. That didn't last though. Following his defeat, it became part of the new Kingdom of Lombardy–Venetia with the Habsburg Emperor Ferdinand of Austria as its king."

"Why are you telling us all this?" Sir Gerald demanded.

"Because when Ferdinand married Maria Anna of Savoy, he had a gift made for her. The Lombardy Jewel."

"What of it?" Sir Gerald insisted.

"In 1866, following Austria's defeat in the Third War of Italian Independence, Lombardy became part of the Kingdom of Italy. And the jewel? It was sold. Today, in Sandham, all these years later, two men are dead because of it."

"Does that bother you?" asked Stefano, somewhat coolly.

"Yes," said Jane, "but you'll recall I mentioned my aunt and myself splitting the proceeds of a sale with Norman West. Right now, that's our main business."

Sir Gerald pointed a finger.

"How can we know you're genuine?"

"It's a fair point," said Beatrice.

"I think it's time we met our missing friend," said Jane. "Norman?"

There was a brief moment of hush before Norman West emerged from a rather small cupboard in the sales office and entered the main room. Kate hoped Jane's credibility would now be strengthened.

"Why have you been hiding all week?" Max Drexler asked.

Norman raised an eyebrow.

"I'm sure I didn't imagine William Benson's body at the cottage. Somebody killed him. Somebody here, most likely."

"Who do you think it was?" asked Stefano.

Norman looked around.

"I'm not sure."

Jane eyed him. "You definitely had a buyer for the jewel though?"

"Yes, Sir Gerald's a liar. He absolutely agreed to buy the jewel. And in case that fell through, I had a trusted back-up buyer – Thomas Smith."

"Take a seat then, Norman," said Jane, "and we'll get on with it."

She carefully removed the Lombardy Jewel from its bag, held it up for a few moments, and placed it on the podium in front of her.

The room was utterly silent, waiting on Jane's next words.

"Who'll start the bidding?" she said. "Shall we say five hundred pounds?"

Sir Gerald Clifton raised a hand.

Thirty-Eight

Glances were exchanged between many of those present. While Sir Gerald seemed determined, others seemed struck by a degree of confusion.

Then Stefano spoke.

"One thousand."

"Thank you," said Jane from the podium. "That's one thousand pounds. Any advance on one thousand?"

"This is most irregular," Peter protested.

"The jewel's worth ten thousand," Jane pointed out. "All you need do is decide how much to bid."

"And what if I refuse?"

"The jewel *will* be sold," said Jane. "In the next few seconds if there's no further interest."

"This is preposterous!" said Peter. "The jewel belongs to my family."

Disbelief rippled through the gathering.

Stefano turned to Beatrice.

"You're Viscountess Lamberg?"

"She is not!" fumed Teresa Alvaro. "I'm Viscountess Lamberg. The jewel belongs to me."

"You?" questioned Stefano.

"It does not belong to you, *Miss* Alvaro!" blasted Beatrice. "You should take your lover-boy and leave!"

Max Drexler said nothing.

"Er, fifteen hundred pounds," said Sir Gerald, trying to catch Jane's eye.

"Yes, thank you, Sir Gerald. The bid is fifteen hundred. Going once…"

Peter scowled. "This is crazy."

"Fifteen hundred pounds. Going twice…"

"Two thousand," said Peter.

Stefano turned to face him.

"I thought you weren't going to bid?"

"You must have misunderstood."

"Peter Langham has bid two thousand pounds for the Lombardy Jewel."

"Two and a half!" declared Sir Gerald Clifton.

Jane raised her gavel. "That's two and a half with Sir Gerald. Norman told me you agreed to pay four thousand when you struck your original deal."

Sir Gerald looked edgy.

"That deal died with Benson. I'm not paying more than I need to."

"Then you are ahead."

"It belongs to me," said Teresa.

"Do I hear three thousand?" said Jane. "I'll remind you once again, it's worth ten."

She was met with muttering.

"Then it's with Sir Gerald Clifton at two and a half thousand. Going once… going twice… are we all done? At two and a half thousand pounds…" She brought the hammer down. "Gone! The Lombardy Jewel is yours, Sir Gerald, at two and a half thousand pounds."

"Good," said Sir Gerald. "I'm glad that's all settled."

"It's just as well," said Jane. "Your money is less than a quarter of a mile away, probably under a hotel mattress."

Kate nodded to him. "Good job you didn't put it in the safe."

"No," said Peter Langham. He pulled a gun from his pocket and stepped out in front. "I've had enough of this nonsense. The jewel belongs to my family. My grandfather bought it directly from the Austrian royal family."

Teresa Alvaro rose to her feet.

"He may have bought it from the royal family, but forty years on, my late husband bought it."

"He had no right to do that. My Grandfather was beset by gambling debts."

"That's unfortunate. Perhaps he was a fool for gambling."

"Oh, he was a fool alright. A fool for living in Monte Carlo. He couldn't handle the casinos. He also lost three houses and a yacht. But your late husband took advantage of him."

"Hans was an honest buyer. Unlike anyone here."

"How dare you," countered Sir Gerald.

Kate assessed the situation.

"Mr Langham, might I suggest you put the gun away."

Peter baulked. "Mr Langham…? Is that what you see. While Miss Alvaro married to gain a title, my name is Peter Leopold Hofmann Gotthard. My ancestor was almost certainly Leopold the Second, Holy Roman Emperor, King of Hungary and Bohemia, and Archduke of Austria."

Kate shrugged. "*Almost* certainly?"

"Enough of this," said Teresa. "My name is Teresa Alvaro, 4th Viscountess of Salmeda."

Max looked up at her.

"With respect, Lady Salmeda, this is not the time."

"No, this is very much the time. I didn't marry for a title. I have my own in the Peerage of Spain, granted by Alfonso the Twelfth to my great-grandfather, a winemaker to royalty."

Kate was intrigued. "From Miss Alvaro to a viscountess twice over."

"When I married Hans von Lamberg, yes. The House of Lamberg is an ancient Austrian noble family."

Peter laughed. "Which makes my point. The Lombardy Jewel belongs to Austria. You are Spanish. Your rights died with your husband."

"Nonsense," said Teresa. "The Spanish ruled Lombardy long before the Austrians."

Beatrice was aghast. "You're to marry an Englishman! One who fought in the War against the Empire!"

"The War is in the past," said Teresa.

Now Stefano stood up.

"Everyone knows the Austrian nobility ceased to exist after the War."

"Your opinion is meaningless," said Peter.

"Oh really? In the summer of 1866, my great-grandfather was a proud Italian who lost his life chasing the Austrians out of Lombardy."

Sir Gerald huffed. "It sounds like the Empire's still at war."

Kate shrugged. "In the matter of the Lombardy Jewel – yes."

Peter raised his gun.

"Let's bring this discussion to an end, shall we?"

Beatrice grabbed the jewel from the podium.

"I'll have the back door key too," she said.

Kate handed it over.

"I assume your hired boat is waiting for you at the quayside."

"A hop, skip and a jump from here, yes."

Peter pointed the gun at Stefano.

"No heroics, Passoni."

"Is it even loaded?" demanded Stefano through gritted teeth.

Peter turned the gun away and fired, shattering the head of Julius Caesar.

Then the bearded man stood up and pointed a gun.

And so did Max Drexler.

Thirty-Nine

Between Kate and Jane, specks of dust could be seen floating in the low sunlight coming through the windows. It was a moment suspended in time. Two guns were trained on Peter Langham, while his was pointing at Kate. She hoped it was because she was nearest and that he didn't hold a specific grudge.

"Is anyone going to say anything?" she wondered. "Because somebody needs to!"

Jane fixed her gaze on Peter.

"What kind of coward are you? Pointing a gun at an unarmed woman?"

Peter turned the gun on Jane.

"Be quiet."

The moment of silence returned, but only briefly.

"Right!" said the bearded man. He pulled his beard off and removed his hat and spectacles. "I'm Inspector

Leonard Ridley of Scotland Yard. My colleague is Inspector Jens Dorn of the Swiss police. Mr Langham, put the gun down."

Peter's eyes darted from here to there looking for a way out.

"Put it down," said Beatrice. "You've done nothing wrong."

"You're right, of course. I've done nothing wrong."

Slowly, he placed the gun on the auctioneer's podium, where Jane quickly pulled it away.

Ridley came down to the front. "Mrs Forbes, if you wouldn't mind unbolting the back door. I have some men outside."

Kate did so and let in Sergeant Jones and Constables Harris and Edmonds. They were followed by three more uniformed men who had come over from Brighton to assist.

"Now then," said Ridley, "Mr Langham, if you wouldn't mind sitting down while we sort this mess out."

"I was merely attempting to stop the theft of an Austrian heirloom."

"Liar," murmured Stefano Passoni.

"Alright, that's enough," Ridley insisted. "Let's have a bit of quiet."

"Good work, inspector," Sir Gerald Clifton enthused. He looked pleased with himself. "As you've no doubt deduced, I was attempting to trick those villainous women into selling the jewel to me. I, of course, would have handed it over to the police immediately."

"I'm not interested. Two men are dead and I want answers."

Max Drexler, now identified as Inspector Dorn, stepped into the discussion.

"As far as I can see, we have three suspects for murder. The international con artist and thief, Stefano Passoni; the international playboy who lives on the proceeds of crime, Peter Langham; and Sir Gerald Clifton, the custodian of many stolen artefacts, including items from Tutankhamun's tomb we would like to retrieve."

Sir Gerald's cry of "rubbish!" could just about be heard above Stefano and Peter's protests of innocence.

"Sir Gerald's the killer," Peter insisted. "Benson wouldn't give him the jewel, so he struck him with a poker."

"I wasn't even there!"

"Yes, you were. And then you killed Tanner!"

Sir Gerald turned to the gathering. "I wasn't near the boat house, but I did send my man Tanner to deter Peter from trying to get the jewel."

Peter scoffed. "Then *you* killed Benson and *Stefano* must have killed Tanner!"

"Nonsense!" cried Stefano, "I was merely following Tanner hoping he would lead me to Norman. Then I lost him among the tourists. When I tried the boat house, I found Mrs Forbes and Lady Jane!"

"I can explain what happened," said Jane. Her voice wasn't as loud, but its conviction cut through the babble. "With your permission, inspector."

"Please do continue."

"Thank you."

There was a moment of quiet and expectation before Jane spoke again.

"Now, we know Teresa Alvaro, or more properly, Lady Salmeda, discovered the Lombardy Jewel missing in Paris. It wasn't her being in Paris that interested me though. It was how she got there. She arrived on the Orient Express."

"That's right," said Lady Salmeda.

"You see, this was never about Paris. It was about Vienna. Mr Langham, how was the recent Mozart recital? Sung in German, wasn't it? I understand you and your sister had seats near the president. I telephoned the opera house to get the date of the performance. It was the evening before Lady Salmeda ended a visit to her late husband's family, also in Vienna, and travelled to Paris by train."

Peter scowled. "That's not proof of anything."

"You hired someone to steal the jewel for you before Lady Salmeda could take it to London."

"You can't possibly know that."

"I've cross-referenced what I know with Inspector Dorn. Had you been the thief, there would have been a danger of her seeing you on the train. No, you paid someone, but your plan backfired. Whatever you were paying this thief, they decided they could get more by selling the jewel themselves."

"Nonsense."

"You're an experienced criminal. You know the international market. Once you realised you'd been double-crossed, you knew where to ask questions. You learned the jewel was coming to Sir Gerald Clifton via William Benson and Norman West. You hired a boat and got here first."

"It's not true."

"It sounds true to me," said Stefano.

Jane continued. "By then, an officer working for an international police organization had been tipped off by an informant and raced to get here, followed by the jewel's owner. But you were ahead of Benson. You watched him. You followed him. He was waiting at Sea View Cottage for Norman West but saw you coming up the path. He smelt a rat and hid the jewel."

"I really don't know anything about it. Inspector, I urge you to intervene."

Ridley remained stony-faced, so Jane continued.

"Mr Langham, you murdered William Benson with a poker."

Peter scoffed. "You simply have no proof!"

"Not at first, no. But we do now. Inspector Ridley?"

Ridley retrieved the bullet from his pocket and held it up.

Peter protested. "A bullet? You can't solve a murder by identifying the wrong weapon."

"You pulled a gun on Benson. There was a struggle. The gun went off and shot a bullet through the rug into the floorboard. The gun fell to the floor, so you grabbed the nearest available makeshift weapon – a poker by the fireplace."

"That's not what happened."

"By the way, thanks for producing the gun. You weren't worried about bringing it, were you – after all, the police were looking into two blunt instrument murders. The bullet you just fired will be a match for the one I found at the cottage."

"Alright… I admit I was at the cottage."

All fell silent. And Kate wondered – was this a confession? Had they got their man?

Peter pressed on. "Yes, I spoke to Benson. I even threatened him by firing a warning shot. But then I left. Clifton or Tanner or Norman West must have killed him."

Now it was Jane who pushed on.

"Next, we had a second murder. Frederick Tanner had worked out who killed Benson. He asked to meet you, Mr Langham. No doubt he left a message or a note for you. You went to see him on the harbour shore. Who would notice you there strolling and talking. But then an opportunity to make it more private presented itself. No doubt, in the boat house, Tanner threatened you. He told you to leave or he'd inform the police. His only objective was to clear a path for his boss, Sir Gerald. I dare say you were caught on the hop, without a gun. You had to improvise. Hence a bash over the head with an oar."

"It's true," said Sir Gerald Clifton. "I can confirm that Peter Langham killed poor Freddie."

Peter railed. "You're not fit to comment. You're a crook and a liar."

"Mr Langham," said Jane, "you were seen at the time of Tanner's murder."

For a moment, Peter froze.

He then regained his composure.

"You're going to tell me someone saw me rowing nearby. It's true. It means nothing."

Jane gave it a moment before responding.

"When Tanner was murdered, a local old-timer saw you going into the boat house and then leaving."

"A witness?" Peter questioned.

Jane's gaze was steadfast.

"Yes, a witness."

"But… I…"

"Everything you planned has unravelled. You were seen going into and leaving that boat house at the exact moment Tanner was killed. It's over."

"No…"

Kate studied Peter's eyes. Perhaps he was seeing Ned Dawson talking with her and Jane. Perhaps he was trying to work out another excuse.

But Beatrice cut in.

"Peter… oh, you're such a fool! We should have left after you killed Benson, but you couldn't step back. I've always known your greed would be our downfall. And now look at us!"

Peter's rage exploded.

"Benson should have handed the jewel over! And as for Tanner… how dare a hired thug threaten me!"

Ridley stepped in.

"Peter Langham, I'm arresting you for the murders of William Benson and Frederick Tanner."

Peter tried to make a run for it, but Constable Harris grabbed him and brought him to the floor.

A few moments later, while a subdued Peter and Beatrice were led outside, Sergeant Jones came over to Kate and Jane.

"A witness to the second murder? I'd like a name for this old-timer."

He stood ready, pencil poised over his pad.

Jane smiled patiently.

"Yes, it's Chester… the cat."

Jones slowly raised his eyes.

Kate meanwhile had a thought.

"I wonder if Chester knows he's brought down Peter Leopold Hofmann Gotthard of the Austro-Hungarian Habsburg Empire. We'll have to get him a treat, Jane."

*

While various criminals were taken away, Kate and Jane joined Inspectors Ridley and Dorn, and Lady Salmeda.

There was only a slight disturbance – Norman West protesting that he was an honest broker and that there had obviously been a mistake.

"Reduced sentence? I should be set free!"

"Those were unusual methods, Lady Jane," Dorn pointed out, "but it's a good outcome for cooperation."

Jane looked relieved. "Thanks for playing along."

Lady Salmeda smiled. "Someone was about to get away with murder. Once Inspector Ridley explained your idea, we felt it was worth a try."

"I have to confess I wasn't in favour at first," Dorn confirmed, "but without your plan, we would have only Norman West or whatever he calls himself."

"It ended well," said Lady Salmeda. "That's what matters. I can't tell you the frustration I had trying to get information out of Inspector Dorn."

Kate smiled. She was sorry for thinking they were having an affair and felt it was probably best to omit mentioning it in her statement.

"It just leaves the question of the insurance company's reward," said Ridley. "I hear it's three hundred pounds."

Dorn was certain. "It goes to Mrs Forbes and Lady Jane. There can be no doubt!"

Jane smiled. "Aunt Kate and I have already discussed it. We'd like the money to go to the police rehabilitation home in Hove."

Ridley's eyes widened.

"Oh… what a gesture." He seemed genuinely stunned. "On behalf of all police officers, thank you."

"That's all agreed then," said Kate. "Everything's worked out perfectly."

"Not quite, Aunt. What about poor Julius Caesar?"

"Ah yes, I was rather keen on buying that. Still, I never really had room on my shelf."

"You have now," said Jane. "Without a head, it'll fit perfectly!"

Forty

Jack Wilson brought the hammer down on the sale of a silver cutlery set. It was a packed house for the auction of the Brand family's effects.

Kate and Jane were standing at the back as all thirty seats had been taken within seconds of the building opening. Now, half an hour in, Mr Wilson's brisk approach had raced through dozens of lots – meaning the sole item of interest to Kate was drawing ever closer to its moment.

It would be a good day. Not just the auction, but a rescheduled lunch at Lady Davenport's. Obviously, it would be a better day if Kate could land the vase.

Just then, Inspector Ridley broke through the crowd to join them.

"I thought I'd say goodbye."

"You didn't have to, inspector," said Kate.

"Well, I wanted to say thank you once again. You both made my job a lot easier."

Jane laughed. "Good acting, inspector. Your 'bearded man' was a triumph. Good job the Alhambra Theatre had a few spare beards. And it was very sporting of the real chap to lend you his hat and glasses."

Ridley smiled. "*And* his suit and tie. I had an idea some of the suspects might have caught a glimpse of him around town. Criminals are suspicious of everyone, so I thought they'd accept that I was a crook too – and having Norman name me as a back-up buyer definitely helped. Mind you, I did once appear on stage in 'A Christmas Carol' at school. I was seven."

"I assume you'll have company on the train," said a smiling Kate.

"Yes, I've got a couple of men down from Scotland Yard to accompany myself, Inspector Dorn and Lady Salmeda. We're taking Peter Langham and Beatrice Fry back to London. Sir Gerald Clifton and Stefano Passoni have been taken to Brighton."

"Not for a day out, I hope."

"Oh, there's no sea view where they're being held. Nor in the cell at Sandham, where Norman's still complaining of a misunderstanding – despite the fact he'll get a reduced sentence."

"Peter Langham…" Jane mused. "He was the one."

"Yes, Peter Leopold Hofmann Gotthard," said Ridley. "Mind you, he added Gotthard to his name. Apparently, it was the family name of some emperor he thought he might possibly be related to. I dunno, Spanish Habsburgs,

Austrian Habsburgs… that family was spread over most of Europe."

Jane laughed. "That family *ruled* most of Europe."

"The thing is, Langham had enough money for a comfortable life. It was just never enough for him. An overblown sense of entitlement there, that's for sure."

"He's facing justice now," said Kate. "That's what matters. We can thank your international colleague too."

"Yes, the cat's out of the bag. We British are joining the International Criminal Police Commission."

"I saw the headline," said Kate. "*International Police Solve Sandham Conspiracy.* It's amazing how fast news travels these days."

She skipped over Colin Nelson's only mention of them in the entire article – *'the police were assisted by Lady Jane Scott and an elderly relative.'*

"It's a good system," said Ridley. "Telephone calls between Scotland Yard, Vienna, Paris… putting together the remaining pieces. Stefano Passoni is a gentleman thief who pops up all over Europe. He was onto the jewel as soon as it went missing. Last night, police raided his Paris flat. A number of stolen items were recovered, so that's him done for. We did our bit too. With Sir Gerald Clifton implicated in a murder inquiry, we were able to get a warrant to search his house. We found several forged Hatherley's receipts for stolen items in his collection. All signed by Reginald Unsworth."

"International police operations," Kate enthused. "It sounds exciting."

"Exciting?" Ridley frowned. "You should see the paperwork."

"Who knows, inspector," said Jane, "perhaps you'll soon be travelling all over Europe in the fight for justice."

"I hope not. Mind you, I'm in the minority. There's a big conference in Switzerland coming up in September. Scotland Yard, the Home Office – they're all fighting each other to go."

"Really?" said Kate. "Who's going to be running the Yard while they're all away?"

Ridley laughed.

Just then, Inspector Dorn and Lady Salmeda joined them. Kate welcomed them warmly and added an important update.

"International conspiracies aside, I have my eye on a vase. It could be tough going though."

"I'm sure you can handle any tough going," said Inspector Dorn. "For example, I hear you might seek to become a town representative?"

"Jane thinks I should," said Kate.

Ridley agreed. "Yes, hopefully, it'll keep you out of trouble."

"We'll see, although it does have its appeal."

But suddenly, her eyes were aflame.

"This is it!"

Jack Wilson's assistant was holding aloft a special item as Jack himself swung into action.

"What am I bid for this mid-last century vase? Do I hear ten shillings? Anyone? That's ten shillings… come on, ten bob… half a pound… anyone?"

Kate's hand snaked upward.

"Thank you, Mrs Forbes. Ten shillings I'm bid. Do I hear twelve?"

From a front seat, Ernie Melton's hand shot up.

"Twelve bob, thank you, Mr Melton. Do I hear fifteen?"

It was a tense atmosphere, at least from Kate's perspective. Perhaps others were more relaxed. Once again, she signalled her intent…

"Fifteen shillings, thank you."

… followed by Ernie Melton doing likewise.

"That's seventeen shillings. Thank you. Mr Melton. Do I hear a whole pound? Come on, twenty shillings… a bargain… anyone?"

Kate hesitated. Should she bid a pound? Ernie Melton might bid more. And then where would she be?

"Mrs Forbes?"

This was getting serious. Even Jane looked concerned.

"What will you do, Aunt?"

Kate turned to Inspector Ridley.

"That man at the front… he could be part of an international vase gathering gang. Perhaps you should take him away for questioning."

"Well, it's a lovely vase, that's for sure. I think Mrs Ridley would like that. I might have to make a bid myself."

Kate tensed up. "Don't you dare!"

But Ridley could only chuckle.

"Do I hear one pound?" Jack Wilson asked.

"Yes, a pound," Kate confirmed.

"One pound, two shillings!" cried Ernie.

This was personal. No doubt about it.

"Two pounds!" came a new bid.

Kate looked past Inspector Ridley to Lady Salmeda's raised hand. From the front, Ernie Melton was doing likewise.

"Two pounds I'm bid. By…?"

"Lady Salmeda. I'll bid ten if I have to."

Ernie Melton slumped down in his chair.

"Sold! Two pounds! Thank you. Next item, please."

As Jack Wilson's assistant held aloft a silver toast rack, Kate turned to Lady Salmeda again.

"Well, congratulations. It's a lovely vase."

"And it's yours, Mrs Forbes. My pleasure."

Kate was gobsmacked.

"Oh, thank you. That's very generous!"

Teresa took the money from her purse and handed it over.

"Well, we'll be off," said Ridley. "Mind how you go."

Farewells and best wishes were exchanged. Then they were gone.

"We should go too," said Jane. "I quite fancy a paddle in the sea before we go to Lady Davenport's for lunch."

A thrilled Kate smiled. As for the vase – she would pick it up later.

On the way down Royal Avenue, with the sea up ahead, Jane gave her aunt's hand a squeeze.

"I think I mentioned a dig at Penford Priory in September."

"You did."

"Why don't you come along. You could stay overnight."

"Thank you, Jane, but you might want to spend the time there with genuine enthusiasts."

"I know you worry about my future, so I want you to meet some of my colleagues. I want you to see me with them, happy and fulfilled. It's important to me."

Kate felt a warm glow. A year on from Henry's passing, loneliness was being challenged by these precious chances for renewal. Would she ever be the best aunt possible? Perhaps not – but that wasn't the point. It was doing her best that mattered. Simply that.

"Jane, I would love to come along. Thank you."

"Brilliant. Hopefully, you'll take a shine to Harry. He's Professor Nash's assistant."

Kate looked askance at her niece. And there it was – the slightest hint of a blush that was gone in a flash.

"Well… how interesting, Jane."

Her niece laughed and squeezed Kate's hand again.

"Actually, Aunt, I've been meaning to ask. The Penford Priory dig is in September, but I'd love you to come up to

London before then. We could do some shopping and try out a couple of new restaurants. How does that sound?"

"Jane..." Kate felt her heart swell. "Honestly, I can't wait!"

The End (Until Next Time...)

If you enjoyed Kate and Jane's second adventure, it would be incredibly helpful if you could leave a review on Amazon. A few words would be fine. Your support genuinely makes a difference by encouraging more people to take a chance on these stories.

*

Don't miss the next book in the series:

"The Body at Penford Priory"

England, September 1928

When Kate visits Jane at an archaeological dig, both are hoping to discover evidence of Medieval life.

What they don't expect to encounter is a body buried only twenty years ago, a perplexing mystery, and the arrival of Inspector Ridley from Scotland Yard.

*

For details of books by B. D. Churston please visit the website.

www.churstonmysteries.com